The Kingdom of God Is Like…

Patricia C. Friel

Dedication

This book is dedicated to my husband, John. He is so very supportive of all my writing efforts and the outreach I am involved in with all areas of our community. He is always willing to go with me in response to those calls in the middle of the night that come from people in need.

Acknowledgment

There are so many people who have been an encouragement to bring this book to print. Professors who know my work have read and encouraged the writing of this book. Pastor friends and mentors have also encouraged my literary endeavors over the years. I also want to thank Mike Turner of Parker Publishers for reaching out to me and offering to publish this book. The staff of Parker Publishers has been phenomenal to work with, and includes Betsy Williams, Executive Editorial Director, and Sandy Stevens, Senior Project Manager. Sandy was quietly insistent and kept the project moving forward in a timely fashion. I cannot thank the Lord enough for bringing this publishing company into my life.

Table of Contents

Introduction

We often hear the phrase, "I am a disciple/follower of Christ." Do we really know what we are saying? It has been my observation that many times we say we are disciples of Christ when in reality we are disciples of the world we live in and look at ourselves, others, and events through that mindset. A very simple definition of disciple is "one who follows and learns from a teacher." As disciples of Jesus, we learn from him and do our best to obey his commandments and teachings.

Some of the most basic commands that Jesus taught are found in the gospel accounts:

You shall love the Lord your God with all your heart, with all your soul, and with all your mind…You shall love your neighbor as yourself. Matthew 22:37, 39

Love your enemies and pray for those who persecute you. Matthew 5:44

Patricia C. Friel

Love one another. Just as I have loved you, you should also love one another. John 13:34

A disciple learns by spending time with the teacher; therefore, the disciple needs to go where the teacher goes and do what the teacher does. How did Jesus live out the basic commands listed above, and how does he expect his followers to do the same? Luke 15:2 tells us that on several occasions, the religious leaders of Jesus' day complained to his disciples because Jesus *"welcomes the sinners and eats with them."* Jesus' response was *"Those who are well have no need of a physician, but those who are sick..."* (Luke 5:31)

The goal of being a disciple of Jesus is to see transformation in people's lives. Discipleship is the life we live with Christ and our fellow disciples as we live out the Kingdom of Heaven/the Kingdom of God, as Jesus taught and demonstrated while on earth. Disciples of Jesus have the same ability to bring the Kingdom of Heaven/the Kingdom of God into people's lives through the power of the Holy Spirit, which was first given on Pentecost. That same Holy Spirit is still within us today, doing the same for us as for the early followers of Jesus. The Holy Spirit leads disciples to be obedient to Jesus' commandments and empowers them to employ their gifts for ministry with and for the Kingdom of God on earth.

I pray that the following pages offer insight and a challenge to become obedient disciples of the Lord Jesus Christ, so that more and more people are reached with the good news of the kingdom of heaven.

What is the Good News? Luke 4:16-18 tells us that disciples bring *"good news to the poor, release to the captives, open the eyes of the blind [both spiritually and physically], and liberate the oppressed."* Matthew 25:37-40 goes on to say, *".... feed the hungry, give a drink to the thirsty, clothe the naked, welcome the stranger, and visit the sick and prisoners."*

The people Jesus associated with and ministered to were the outcasts, the marginalized, the blind, the deaf, the depressed, the religious, those who were seeking. In other words, he ministered to all those who needed to hear about God's kingdom and how to experience new life while still in the throes of living out a normal lifespan on earth.

To help us understand how we can be disciples and do as Jesus did more impactfully, we need to know more about the Kingdom of heaven/Kingdom of God that Jesus said was possible to bring to earth. We need to know, understand, and practice the Kingdom of heaven as Jesus did when he walked the earth. Jesus promised in John 14:12, *"Very truly I tell you, whoever believes in me will do the works I have been doing, and they will do even greater things than these, because I am going to the Father."*

Are you ready to accept the challenge to do even greater works than Jesus did? In John 14:15-21, Jesus tells his disciples:

Patricia C. Friel

If you love me, keep my commands. And I will ask the Father, and he will give you another advocate to help and be with you forever – the Spirit of Truth. The world cannot accept him, because it neither sees him nor knows him, but he lives with you and will be in you [or is in you]. Whoever has my commands and keeps them is the one who loves me. The one who loves me will be loved by my Father, and I, too, will love them and show myself to them.

Chapter 1:
God Created

The understanding of who God is, what He desires, and how He chooses to accomplish His will on earth as it is in heaven precedes an understanding of how He feels about us, His creation. The very first chapter of Genesis, verses one through two, states, *"In the beginning God created the heavens and the earth. Now the earth was without form and empty, darkness was over the surface of the deep, and the Spirit of God was hovering over the waters."* Another way to consider how the earth was is to consider words such as chaos, darkness, and emptiness.

For whatever reason, God above all gods chose to create sacred space with sacred food and animals for a sacred humankind. This can be readily seen with the information the rest of Genesis chapter one provides. God only had to speak, and everything came into being: day/night, sky/earth, seas/dry land, all the vegetation upon the earth, sun/moon, birds/fish, the domesticated animals/wild animals. After each spoken creative act, God made the pronouncement that it was good. God gave instructions to His creative acts. All plant, marine, animal, and avian life were given the ability to procreate after their own kind.

God then says in Genesis 1:26, *"Let us make mankind in our image, in our likeness, so they may rule over the fish in the sea, and the birds in the sky, over the livestock and all the wild animals, and over all the creatures that move along the ground."* Remember, God spoke all that He created into existence. However, looking at Genesis 2:7, a different creative act is undertaken by God. *"Then the LORD God formed a man from the dust of the ground and breathed into his nostrils the breath of life, and the man became a living being."* Genesis 2:22 then tells of how woman was created: *"Then the LORD God made a woman from the rib He had taken out of the man, and He brought her to the man."* Therefore, the human race was not spoken into existence, but by the very personal hand of God they were created. Just as a sculptor might fashion a person, so God had a "hands-on" approach in creating humanity. Unlike a sculptor who leaves the person that was created lifeless, just something to look upon and admire, the LORD God Himself, according to Genesis 2:7, *"...breathed into his nostrils the breath of life, and the man became a living being."* God had a very intimate relationship with humanity from our very inception.

The question then becomes, why did God speak all things into existence, but humankind was created by His personal touch and breath? People often say God created humanity for relationships. However, Genesis 1:28 says this, *"…be fruitful and increase in number; fill the earth and subdue it. Rule over the fish in the sea and the birds in the sky, and over every living creature that moves on the ground."* The God who spoke and created had all authority, power, and dominion over everything. Yet, He chose to share some of that with humanity. He had a job for them [and us] to do. Psalm 8 reminds us of the creation story. In verse 5, the psalmist says that God *"made them [us/humanity] a little lower than the angels.* [The word in Hebrew is elohim, according to Strong's Concordance. This suggests that God made us a little lower than Himself.] Verse 6 goes on to say, *"You made them rulers over the works of your hands; you put everything under their feet."* We will return to this thought further in chapter ten of this book.

As we continue to examine scripture and how we become disciples of Jesus, we will discuss how humanity can reclaim the power, authority, and dominion that were given to them at the very beginning.

The story continues with Genesis 2:8 stating, *"Now the LORD God had planted a garden in the east, in Eden; and there He put the man He had formed."* The boundaries of the Garden of Eden were the four rivers named in Genesis 2:11-14, the Pishon, the

Gihon, the Tigris, and the Euphrates. This perfect garden needed to be cared for, and God created a perfect humanity to care for the garden. The garden contained all that man needed to sustain life, and He put Adam in the garden "to work it and take care of it." As can be seen, the Garden of Eden was not the whole earth that God spoke into being. It was a small portion of the planet with certain rivers as boundaries. Adam had authority, dominion, and power over that portion of the earth. So, what happened? How did mankind lose authority, power, and dominion over even a small portion of its world?

Genesis three starts the story of Eve's encounter with the serpent and proceeds with Adam eating the fruit of the Tree of Knowledge of Good and Evil. Because of that act of disobedience on Adam's part, God pronounced judgment on how the man and woman would now have to live. To the woman, God said, *"I will make your pains in childbearing very severe; with painful labor you will give birth to children. Your desire will be for your husband to rule over you.* (Genesis 3:16). Amazingly, God made a definite distinction between Adam and Eve. He told Adam, *"Because you listened to your wife and ate fruit from the tree about which I commanded you, 'You must not eat from it.'"* Then God goes on to pronounce judgment on Adam. As a child who grew up on a small dirt farm, I used to wish that Adam had remained obedient to God and not eaten from the tree that God had commanded him not to eat from. That curse God placed on the ground because of Adam's disobedience also became my curse as my brothers, and I would have to hoe all the weeds and thistles from the corn rows and the garden every summer under a hot, Ohio sun. It was a never-ending task. God told Adam:

Cursed is the ground because of you; through painful toil you will eat food from it all the days of your life. It will produce thorns and thistles for you, and you will eat the plants of the field. By the sweat of your brow, you will eat your food… (Genesis 3:17b-19a).

As scripture tells us, Adam's disobedience separated not only him from God's presence, but that disobedience from the first man has visited humanity from that time forth, until the birth of Jesus. Ask anyone, especially those living in more agrarian, marginalized communities. The curse of the ground is still there today. Women still give birth in great pain, even with the help of modern medicine. The question throughout the ages is how can people regain a relationship, a close connection to their Creator? Anyone with an understanding of anthropology and sociology knows that people have turned to the worship of many things over the ages, which they have called gods. Whether it is the pagan gods of the ancients or the gods of modernity, such as science and money, to name only a few, we are still worshipping something other than our Creator God.

Yet, within every person is a desire, a longing to have something or someone greater than themselves to look to, to emulate, to strive after. The Old Testament is the story of the Israelite nation that God chose, for whatever reason that He alone knows, out of all the peoples of the world, to try and have a right relationship with and who would be an obedient people that they might enjoy His presence. The Old Testament is the story of God's never-ending search for a relationship with an obedient people. No group of people ever remained faithful to the LORD God, their Creator. A few individuals remain outstanding in that respect, as mentioned in the Old Testament and related in the book of Hebrews, chapter 11, in the New Testament.

It is incredible that God has never given up or abandoned the people He created by His hand. The question had to be, "How to restore to humanity the power, authority, and dominion that had been theirs in the beginning?"[1] We must go to the New Testament to answer that question.

---

[1] Cyril of Alexandria (376-444) discusses at length in his sermon on John 20:22 that the Spirit/breath of God into Adam in Genesis 2:7 to be the Holy Spirit whom humanity lost at the fall but was restored at Pentecost. Thus, the question of how the image of God became compromised by sin but can be restored through the Spirit, then dominion is possible by the healing of that image and the restoration of the spirit within all who receive the Spirit of God through Christ Jesus.

Chapter 2:
Visible Versus Invisible

In the last chapter, we were reminded of God's original plan for humanity: to live in harmony with Him, with self, with others, and to rule over the earth. We also learned that God totally supplied everything Adam and Eve needed and had a face-to-face relationship with Him. After the fall, everything changed. Humanity was in total disharmony with God, with self, with others, and with the earth, as Adam had lost his authority over it. At this point, we will accept that the garden's existence cannot be regained in all its perfection until the millennial reign, at the earliest, or until Christ returns and God unfolds the new heaven and new earth, at the latest.

But the Kingdom of God is here now! We do not have to wait until we get to heaven to live a life of peace, joy, security, and abundance. We can have all that in the present. However, we must be aware of two underlying principles:

1. We live in an obvious world ruled by Satan and satanic forces, but God laid down rules from His invisible world (kingdom) that can and will guide us as we live out life on this earth. By obeying God's rules and following His precepts, we can obtain the peace, joy, security, and abundance that were given to us in the beginning.

2. This invisible world, made up of demonic and angelic forces, undergirds, surrounds, and penetrates the visible world. The invisible world impacts the visible world because it does not have the same restrictions and limitations as the visible world. Only humankind, endowed with free will at creation, can make a choice that the unseen world listens to.

Most people, including Christians, think the Kingdom of God will arrive when the new heaven and earth arrive, as Revelation chapters 21 and 22 relate. WRONG! In Matthew 4:17, Jesus said, *"...Repent, for the kingdom of heaven is near."* Also, in Matthew 5:3 from the Sermon on the Mount, we find these words of Jesus, *"Blessed are the poor in spirit, for theirs is the kingdom of heaven..."* Luke 10:9 says, *"Heal the sick in it and say to them, 'The Kingdom of God has come near to you."* And in Luke 17:21, *"Nor will they say, 'Look, here it is' or 'There!' for behold, the Kingdom of God is in the midst of you."* The second half of the evidence of an invisible world is found in Genesis 32:24-31, where we find Jacob contending with a Man he identifies as God. Then, there is the example of Elijah, his servant, and the king of Aram with his army (2 Kings 6:8-23, especially verse 17). Then, there is the well-known story of Shadrach, Meshach, and Abednego found in Daniel 3, with close attention to verses 25 and 28. The story of Acts relates Peter's release from prison by an angel, Acts 12:1-17, especially verses 7-11. These are but a minimal offering of stories from the Bible of the invisible meeting the visible world. Even today, current stories can be found in books or podcasts about the invisible meeting the visible in people's lives.

If we believe the scriptures, then we must look beyond the visible world that we inhabit and pay such close attention to, into the invisible world. From a world of impossibilities into a world of possibilities: *"For all things are possible with God"* (Mark 10:27). From a world of finiteness to a world of infiniteness (Psalm 147:5). From a stance of mortality into a place of immortality (Romans 6:23).

How can we walk and operate in this invisible world? Jesus said, *"to have faith in God"* (Mark 11:22). Jesus told Nicodemus in John 3:5-8:

Very truly I tell you, no one can enter the Kingdom of God unless they are born of water and the Spirit. Flesh gives birth to flesh, but the Spirit gives birth to spirit. You should not be surprised at my saying, 'You must be born again.' The wind blows wherever it pleases. You hear its sound, but you cannot tell where it comes from or where it is going. So it is with everyone born of the Spirit.

First of all, we must be born of the Spirit of God, a new creation on the inside. We must believe and trust God. We must remember God is omnipotent, that is, He has unlimited power and authority (Mark 4:39, John 11:43-44, Psalm 135:6, Daniel 4:35). God is also omniscient, that is, He knows everything about all things and everyone (Psalm 139:1-4, Isaiah 46:9-10, I John 3:20). A third attribute of God is that He is omnipresent. He can always be everywhere at all times (Psalm 139:7-10, Proverbs 15:3). He is the only free, unrestricted being in the universe. Even Jesus said he was obedient to the Father (John 6:38). We must take time to wait before God. Jesus said, "I do nothing apart from the Father" (John 5:30). Matthew 8:5-9, 13 illustrates how this works well. Once God has shown you how to pray, act, or make a decision, do it! It will come to pass as He said. He is God. He knows everything (omniscient). Jesus said in Mark 11:22-24,

Have faith in God. Truly I tell you, if anyone says to this mountain, 'Go, throw yourself into the sea,' and does not doubt in their heart but believes that what they say will happen, it will be done for them. Therefore, I tell you, whatever you ask for in prayer, believe that you have received it, and it will be yours."

In other words, if you become one in the spirit with His Spirit, if you truly have faith, believe in God's absolute sovereignty and mighty power, and agree with His will, then things will happen as they did with the prophets of old and with Jesus and his disciples. God's sovereignty and power that were present at creation will be activated. Paul's prayer in Ephesians 1:18-21 tells us how it is:

And [I pray] that the eyes of your heart [the very center and core of your being] may be enlightened [flooded with light by the Holy Spirit], so that you will know and cherish the hope [the divine guarantee, the confident expectation] to which He has called you, the riches of His glorious inheritance in the saints (God's people), and [so that you will begin to know] what the immeasurable and unlimited and surpassing greatness of His [active, spiritual] power is in us who believe. These are in accordance with the working of His mighty strength which He produced in Christ when He raised Him from the dead and seated Him at His own right hand in the heavenly places, far above all rule and authority and power and dominion [whether angelic or human], and [far above] every name that is named [above every title that can be conferred], not only in this age and world but also in the one to come. (Amplified Bible)

We have a Biblical record of seeing this in action through history. In some instances, there was only obedience on the part of the person without understanding, but God always worked and acted as He said. Some examples include God's command to Noah to build an ark on dry land because of the rain that would be coming (Genesis 6). Another example is when God worked through Moses with the various plagues upon Egypt and led him to the edge of the Red Sea, which parted upon, when Moses, following God's instruction, raised his rod (Exodus 14:21-22). Elijah commanded the rain to dry up for three years (I Kings 17:1 and 18:1). Jesus stated he did nothing but what the Father commanded him to do (John 12:49-50). The Bible is full of these stories. You probably have some out of your life today. Now is the time to pause, remember, and reflect on God's activities in your life – from the invisible to the visible.

God's kingdom works in a predetermined way with specific requisites. These requisites include being born again, learning from Jesus our teacher, and then acting on the principles we have learned. I would like to expand on those three prerequisites. Being born again is just a beginning, not an arrival. For example, children are born but have not arrived; they must learn to live in this world. Rebirth only gets you into God's kingdom. Following Jesus, the greatest teacher, teaches us how to live in and navigate God's kingdom principles. Then, the Great Commission found in Matthew 28:18-20 says we are to make followers and learners, to teach them to follow Christ. Teaching was the central thrust of Jesus' ministry on earth. The Beatitudes in Matthew 5-7 are a small part of what Jesus taught and demonstrated to his disciples. Jesus's disciples were not expected to be the end recipients of all that Jesus taught. They were expected to be doers. They were expected to demonstrate back to him all that he had taught and shown them. Action is the keyword to being a disciple of Jesus. The two stories found in Luke 9:1-2 and 10:1,8, along with the stories of their work as the early church started, which are found in the book of Acts, all demonstrate how disciples are to advance the Kingdom of God on earth.

That brings us to the question of how God's kingdom works. The first thing we acknowledge is that God's kingdom works in abundance. In fact, all of nature shows God's abundance. The sun has never stopped shining and producing heat so that food can grow, the dry ground continues to be fertile so that crops have nutrients, and rain has occurred in season to water the crops. God's kingdom also includes people who have found favor with God. Luke 2:52 says, *"And Jesus kept increasing in wisdom and stature, and in favor with God and man."* David, despite all his human shortcomings, asked God to keep him as the apple of His eye (Psalm 17:8). Abraham was referred to as a *"friend of God"* (2 Chronicles 20:7, Isaiah 41:8, James 2:23). These and others, both in the Old and New Testaments were used of God to advance his kingdom because their hearts were fixed on Him and His principles and precepts. God's kingdom also works on partnership. God has chosen to enter into partnership with those who love Him. This partnership grows as we pray, discern God's will, and then carry it out here on earth. We become obedient to the will of the Father (John 14:12-14).

The question then becomes, why have we not been seeing God's kingdom at work? The first reason is that we have not been speaking in faith. Remember, God spoke creation into existence. Moses spoke, and the Red Sea parted. Elijah spoke, and the heavens closed up for three years and did not rain. He spoke again, and it rained, ending the drought on the land. Christ spoke, the water turned into wine, the blind received sight, the lame walked, and demons left people. Just as Lazarus was raised from the dead, so was the widow of Nain's son. Once we enter into a partnership with God through rebirth, and He speaks a truth to us, we are emboldened by the Holy Spirit to talk after Him. If we do, we shall see and experience miracles, but if we do not, then things do not happen that advance the Kingdom of God.

The apostle Paul said it this way, *"Put on the mind of Christ."*[2] In other words, speak his mind, speak his thoughts, do not be afraid, do not doubt. Remember, *"For God has not given us a spirit of timidity, but of power and love, and discipline."* (2 Timothy 1:7). We can see then that by living in the kingdom as Christ did

---

[2] Commented [JWS11]: In opening ourselves to the Spirit who dwells within us, we have put on the mind of Christ in as much as Paul calls the Spirit the Christ of Christ. Then in the Spirit our lives have a kenotic character that mirrors the Son's condescension in the Incarnation.

on this earth, in the here and now, we can enter back into what humanity lost in the Garden of Eden. We can return to the authority God gave us at creation.

"God created man in His image and said, 'Be fruitful and multiply and increase in number, fill the earth and subdue it. Rule over the fish of the sea and the birds of the air and over every living creature that moves on the ground."

Chapter 3:
Choose Your Enemy

I do not think you will find anyone, Christian or non-Christian, who will disagree with the statement that there is enmity in the world today. The behavioral patterns of people the world over attest to the fact that enmity exists as we no longer, many times, love ourselves, love others, or love God. This enmity often produces disastrous effects in human affairs. The disagreement then between Christians and secularists (that is, the non-Christians of the world) is not over the existence of enmity, but rather in its causes. I think it is essential to discuss these prevailing views, so before we discuss what sin is from the Hebrew perspective and the consequences of sin, here are some viewpoints that attempt to define the reason for enmity.

First of all, there is the dualist.[3] Dualists believe there are two separate entities, usually viewed as equal, but not always. God is the embodiment of the good, and Satan is the embodiment of evil. These two entities are constantly at war within a person, and because both have equal standing, there cannot be a winner, so the person continues to be in conflict within themselves. Another way to consider this is to believe that enmity is physical in origin. They believe the world and everything in it is made of two basic ingredients, matter and spirit. Matter is essentially evil and spirit good. Therefore, humankind, being both matter and spirit, experiences enmity because it cannot free the pure spirit from the tainted matter.

Then there are the enlightened rationalists or the men who influenced "the Age of Reason". [4] In a highly simplistic fashion, they believe enmity is due to incorrect thoughts. They believe that if people can be taught to think right, they will rise above those things which bring them into conflict with themselves, with others,

---

[3] Augustine, in his "Confessions," explores this in great detail, rejecting this dualism and trying to merge Plato's thinking and writings with scripture. This has informed Christian theology for centuries. Isaiah 14:12-15, Ezekiel 28:13-17 inform us of Satan, while 1 John 4:4 tells us who God is.

[4] Men associated with rationalism lived, wrote, and impacted Western thought from the early to mid-seventeenth century. They include such men as René Descartes, Baruch Spinoza, Frances Bacon, Isaac Newton, John Locke, and Immanuel Kant, to name a few. I Thessalonians 5:21 clears this teaching up for us.

and with the world. This type of thinking is currently embedded in many social science courses, science, politics, and religions, including Christianity.

Third is the humanist.[5] Humanist thought elevates human thought, philosophy, and secular interests over the divine. The humanist perspective of today is most likely a revival of the Renaissance humanists, who also often deemphasized religion.[6]

The fourth group is the determinists. The classical belief is that enmity is due to heredity and environment. They believe that people's attitudes toward themselves and others in the world are conditioned by the sociological and biological factors that surround them. They do not take responsibility for their own actions because they believe their actions are the result of circumstances beyond their control. They do not ascribe to the freewill that God has given to all to determine how they will react

---

[5] The humanist philosophy and definition have changed over the years, depending upon the people associated with the movement. Some modern-day famous people associated with this movement include Gloria Steinem, Carl Sagan, Norman Lear, John Dewey, Barney Frank, and Isaac Asimov, to name just a few. Colossians 2:8 and 2 Timothy 3:5 refute this philosophy.

[6] Dana F. Kellerman. New Webster's Dictionary of the English Language, College Edition. (Consolidated Book Publishers: New York, NY, 1975) p. 732. Also, Google Renaissance Humanism, World History Encyclopedia. Accessed August 2, 2025.

to life's interesting encounters with society, religion, government, etc.[7]

Fifth are the God-blamers. They believe enmity is God's fault. They believe God did not create humanity just quite right. A different creative process would have produced a different humankind. God is to blame. He is responsible.[8] In other words, we set ourselves up as God's judge, forgetting that it is He who made us, not vice versa. It is His fault that whatever calamity occurs, it was not our free will to make decisions that caused it. It was God's fault for not making us perfect in the beginning. When did the blame game start? Consider Genesis 3:12 when God asked Adam who told him he was naked, Adam responded, "The woman you put here with me – she gave me some fruit from the tree, and I ate it." The blame game began when disobedience entered humankind.

Lastly, we have Christians. They accept the Bible as the authoritative word on all matters pertaining to life across the spectrum of individual, family, society, and how to worship God.

---

[7] An excellent overview of determinism over the centuries can be found on Google from the Encyclopedia Britannica site if one looks up the word "determinism." Several articles in succession explain the various evolutions of this philosophy. Accessed August 2, 2025

[8] Proverbs 19:3 is the answer to those who want to pass blame onto God for their human choices

Unlike the other viewpoints we have already covered—and there are many more—the believer traces enmity to its root cause—SIN.

What is sin? In the Hebrew sense, sin is nothing more or less than revolt against God. It is humankind throwing God's restraints to the wind. It is mortals who are too busy playing God to listen to God. It is His created ones believing Satan's hideous lie that life is at its best when it has no restrictions placed upon it. It is that driving, violent quest for unrestrained freedom which subordinates God's will to self-will. In reality, it is essentially and principally a revolt against God! It is listening to Satan's deceptive whispers, instead of being obedient to God that leads to sin, just as in the Garden of Eden.

Let us look again at Genesis 2:15-17.

The LORD God took the man and put him in the Garden of Eden to work it and take care of it. And the LORD God commanded the man, 'You are free to eat from any tree in the garden; but you must not eat from the tree of the Knowledge of Good and Evil, for when you eat of it you will surely die.'

The message of the Bible leaves no doubt that Adam and Eve knew the will of God. They both were called to obedience in the garden. Adam received the command from God, and scripture clearly indicates that he had communicated this to his wife, Eve. The question that the serpent asked Eve was, *"Did God really say, 'You must not eat from any tree in the garden?"* The answer Eve gave, *"We may eat fruit from the trees in the Garden, but did say, 'You must not eat fruit from the tree that is in the middle of the garden, and you must not touch it, or you will die,'"* provide enough evidence that we know ignorance of God's will played no part in the 'garden revolt.' The sin committed in the garden was willful, deliberate disobedience. After eating the fruit of the tree, they were both immediately aware they were naked, responsible for their marred destiny. Immediately, they felt shame and experienced guilt, so they hid from God (Genesis 3:1-10). They knew the will of God but disobeyed it.

Chapter 4:
Consequences of Sin

We will now consider the consequences of sin. There are six consequences of sin that we are going to look at. They are:

1. Sin results in enmity/disharmony with God,
2. Sin results in enmity/disharmony with Self,
3. Sin results in enmity/disharmony with Others,
4. Sin results in enmity/disharmony with Nature,
5. Sin results in the misuse of Creation,
6. Sin results in disobedience, revolt, and separation from God as evidenced by guilt and a sense of guilt which gives rise to shame before God.

First, we will look at the issue of sin that results in enmity with God. *"And they heard the sound of the LORD God walking in the garden in the cool of the day, and the man and his wife hid themselves from the presence of the LORD God among the trees of the garden"* (Genesis 3:8). The horror of sin is that it separates the created from the Creator. Fashioned in God's image and made in His likeness, humankind cannot turn its back on heaven's light without destroying itself and its life in the process. So, humanity is endowed with a moral nature and has written upon their hearts and carved, within their being, a sense of responsibility toward God. Suddenly, with disobedience came guilt and shame. Fearful of facing God, Adam and Eve hid from God. Such a change in their relationship was not gradual, but immediate.

Sin also results in enmity within oneself. No one can be what they were designed to be apart from the God who gave us life. Since we are an intermixture of flesh and spirit, we need God as much as we need air to breathe and water to drink. Without God, life degenerates into a purposeless passing through this world. Estranged from God, no one can find themselves. Blind to the things of the spirit, we waste so much time searching for meaning here and for purpose there. All we do is reach dead ends.

Without God, what do we do when fears, frustrations, anxieties, tension, and depression visit us? Unresolved, they live and linger deep within us, and the heart of God's people, designed for contentment, peace, and joy, becomes a sanctuary for conflict and despair. Scripture has said, and human history documents it, that those at odds with God will soon be at odds with themselves as well. Consider the story of King Saul when he disobeyed God and, instead of destroying the Amalekites and everything belonging to them, he kept the king alive, as well as the best of the flocks of the Amalekites. God lifted His Spirit from King Saul (1 Samuel 15:1-26). Next, God had the prophet Samuel anoint David as the next king (1 Samuel 16:7-13). Saul spent the rest of his life trying to kill David (1 Samuel 18:28-29; 19:1-2; 23:7-8). Saul's disobedience had terrible consequences for him. Saul hated himself, and he hated that David had received the anointing he once had from the LORD God. Because of disobedience, guilt, anger, and hatred, Saul opened the door to a tormenting spirit that stayed with him the rest of his life (1 Samuel 19:9).

The third area in which we see the consequences of sin is where sin results in enmity with others. Let us revisit the scene in the Garden of Eden. Listen to this! Does the tone sound familiar? God asks,

Who told you that you were naked? Have you eaten of the tree which I commanded you not to eat?" The man said, "The woman whom you gave to be with me, she gave me fruit of the tree, and I ate." Then the LORD God said to the woman, "What is this that you have done?" The woman said, "The serpent beguiled me, and I ate.

This is a familiar scene to any parent. Whenever you ask two or more children, "Who is responsible?" they give precisely the same kind of answer Adam and Eve gave to God. Adam pointed his finger at Eve, and she, in turn, pointed her finger at the serpent.

You may raise the question, why do we all wish to pass on the responsibility of our actions and blame others for our failures? The reasons are as follows: A sense of guilt is burdensome. It weighs heavily on the human heart. It is painful. It cuts like a knife into our very being. If we do not resolve guilt God's way, through repentance and forgiveness, then we try to do it our way, through blaming others. By displacing our blame on others, we destroy the possibility of having peace and harmony with those around us. If we are not at peace with ourselves, we will find it impossible to be at peace with those around us and with God.[9]

I will let God speak for what happens as a consequence of sin, resulting in enmity/disharmony with nature.

And to Adam God said, "Because you have listened to the voice of your wife, and have eaten of the tree which I commanded you, "you shall not eat of it, cursed is the ground because of you; in toil you shall eat of it all the days of your life; thorns and thistles it shall bring forth to you; and you shall eat the plants of the field. In the sweat of your face, you shall eat your food till you return to the ground, for out of it you were taken; you are dust, and to dust you shall return.

Sin results in the misuse of creation. How sad God must be to see all that He created and gave to humankind to be used for their

---

[9] The English word peace does not do justice to the Hebrew concept of the word Shalom

good and for the support of life to be so mismanaged. God was not cursing the earth to "even the score" with a rebellious people. The curse was a declaration of WHAT WOULD BE because His children had the choice of a beautiful garden, but through disobedience, they had inherited desert land. Now they must live with that choice.

Sin, disobedience, and estrangement, however we choose to label Adam and Eve's actions or our own, result in enmity/disharmony with all things with God, with self, with others, with nature, and with creation.

Sin, disobedience, revolt, and separation result from one of two things. We either suffer from guilt or have a sense of guilt. Guilt is very different from a sense of guilt. Using the two terms in the Biblical sense, we could say that guilt is that which is ascribed to a people or a person by God when His sovereign will has been violated. A sense of guilt is what a person or people feel when they have violated what they think to be God's will,or failed to live up to their own or others expectations.

If we accept the stated definition of the two terms, it becomes immediately evident that any of us can change our feelings toward a sense of responsibility to God and minimize or even eradicate a "sense of guilt." But NO ONE IS ABLE TO DO ANYTHING ABOUT GUILT ITSELF – except through the blood of Jesus Christ.

We will now look briefly at some of the subtle ways we try to diminish the seriousness of sin and destroy a 'sense of guilt.' The suggestion that 'everybody else is doing it' suggests that moral responsibility is changed by mathematics, but not even the new math can do this. Others may say, 'When folks are foolish enough to believe God holds people responsible for their actions, they will naturally feel guilty.' This method suggests that the elimination of God changes moral responsibility. How often have you heard this: "Sure, I have my faults, but they look like virtues beside the actions of other people I know." This method suggests that responsibility is changed by what other people do. This list can go on and on. Some feel a little extra humanitarian effort will even up the score, more work, more play, more social whirling, and you will not have time to think. The one I really love, "How can a person be responsible who did not have a chance? Look at their environment."

Although each of the above-stated methods might help a person reduce their sense of guilt, none of them affects guilt itself. What are we going to do? Has God abandoned us, His ultimate creation? NO! Let us remember the curse He placed on the serpent from Genesis 3:15, *"And I will put enmity between you and the woman, and between your offspring (seed) and hers; he will crush your head, and you will strike his heel."*

And who is this promise concerning? The Christ, God's son. Only through him will we find forgiveness of sin and the removal of all estrangement from God, from ourselves, from others, and from nature and creation. Only God can remove guilt through the blood sacrifice of Jesus on the cross and the power of the resurrection from the grave of Jesus.

Chapter 5:
Out of Your Heart

We know that God has not abandoned His creation nor humankind. The book of Judges ends with the statement, *"In those days there was no king in Israel; each person did what they thought to be right"* (CEB). After a while, the life of drifting began to take a toll on the collective consciousness of the people. They asked God for a king, as the other nations around them had. God decided to give them what they thought they needed. His statement to Samuel was *"…it is not you they have rejected, but they have rejected me as their king."* (1 Samuel 8:7b)

Once again, God heard His children's lament and gave them what they thought they needed. Throughout the rest of the Old Testament history of the Israelites, they continued to do their "own thing, their own way." Still, God did not abandon His created ones. He sent prophets who warned them of the consequences of not trusting in Him, the LORD God Almighty. Instead, as a nation and for the most part, as individual households, they continued in their worship of manmade gods. In a way, they became syncretists. They continued to give voice to the one true God but indulged in the worship of the gods of the nations around them wholeheartedly. Today, we see the same thing happening among people. They give voice to the fact that they believe in God, or a Higher Power, but in reality, their time, money, and other interests are worshipped first. Like the Israelites, they pay lip service to their faith but give legs and voice to everything else.

The hearts of most people have not changed over the ages. Because God is intimately involved with His creation, He sent a few kings whose hearts were turned toward Him, and revivals intermittently took place in the Israelite nation of Judea, the Southern Kingdom. Usually, these revivals did not last for more than one generation. In His love for His people, God allowed them to be subjugated by foreign nations. However, the majority of the people cursed and bellyached about their condition but did not look to God to save and deliver them as He did when they were in slavery in Egypt. Their celebrations of Passover were merely an empty, formalized ritual. It held no real meaning for their lives and the realization of the providence of a caring God.

It is incredible that when Daniel was delivered from the lion's den, it had more impact on a pagan ruler than on the Hebrew people at the time. God used a true worshipper/believer to work through and change a Gentile heart. It could be said that Daniel was a disciple of the One True God, so God was able to display His power and dominion to save Daniel from the lion's mouth. That visible miracle changed a king's heart and saved a nation (story found in Daniel 6). The story of Daniel's faith in the God of Israel made its way from King Darius to his successor, King Cyrus. Under King Cyrus, Ezra was allowed to return to Jerusalem with a remnant of the Jewish people to rebuild the promised land. Faith in God has an impact, not just on immediate circumstances, but also has a far-reaching impact on people and even nations.

God is always present. God is always active. God is always willing to prove to His created ones who He really is. It is on us that we choose to either totally ignore Him or else limit who He is, what His abilities are, by who we are, and what our abilities are. God took pity on humanity. In the fullness of time, He provided a more "in your face" voice to call people across the nations to Him.

At this point in the story of God's action on the part of His created ones, we will move to the New Testament.

God even went so far as to prepare people's hearts to receive the truth that He alone was God and that He loved His creatures. God wanted people to know Him intimately and live the abundant, fruitful life He had created us to live from the very beginning. He sent John the Baptist to prepare the way for His own coming into the world. When you think in farming terms, John the Baptist came to plow the ground and break up the hard clods of people's hearts, to soften them so that when the seed was planted, it would have the appropriately prepared soil in which to take root and grow. John the Baptist came to call a lost people to repentance, to turn from ignoring God's laws and indulging in mindless religious practices to looking into their hearts and repenting of sinful thoughts, deeds, and practices.

In the fullness of time, God sent His Son, Jesus, into the world so that all could hear and learn firsthand how the Creator wanted things to be in His kingdom. People would no longer have the excuse to say they do not know what God requires, or what His precepts and principles are. They could no longer say they did not understand kingdom rule and authority. However, knowing the Father's heart, teaching the Father's heart, and demonstrating the Father's heart do not guarantee the hearer will be obedient to the Father's heart, for God gave free will to humankind. Jesus did all that the Father required him to do. Judas Iscariot, with whom most people are familiar as the betrayer of Jesus to the Jewish rulers, is an example of someone who personally knew Jesus, heard the teachings of Jesus, and was sent on ministry work to the Jewish people, yet was the betrayer (Matthew 10:1-4). Where is your free will taking you on this spiritual journey?

The Living Bible translation quotes Paul's thoughts in both Galatians and Colossians,

But when the right time came, the time God decided on, He sent His Son, born of a woman, born as a Jew, to buy freedom for us who were slaves to the law so that he could adopt us as his very own sons [daughters]. And because we are his sons [daughters], God has sent the Spirit of his Son into our hearts, so now we can rightly speak of God as our dear Father. Now we are no longer slaves but God's own sons [daughters]. And since we are his sons [daughters], everything he has belongs to us, for that is the way God planned. (Galatians 4:4-7)

Christ is the exact likeness of the unseen God. He existed before God made anything at all, and, in fact, Christ himself is the Creator who made everything in heaven and earth, the things we can see and the things we can't; the spirit world with its kings and kingdoms, its rulers and authorities; all were made by Christ for his own use and glory. He was before all else began, and it is his power that holds everything together. He is the Head of the body made up of his people – that is, his Church – which he began; and he is the Leader of all those who arise from the dead, so that he is first in everything; for God wanted all of himself to be in his Son. It was through what his Son did that God cleared a path for everything to come to him – all things in heaven and on earth – for Christ's death on the cross has made peace with God for all by his blood. (Colossians 1:15-20)

Patricia C. Friel

As can be seen, God decides when events will occur in this world. He is not a God who created and then sat back to see how His created ones on this earth would come out. He is intimately involved. Yet, we do not enter His invisible world to know how to go about His business in the visible world. Jesus showed us how that was possible.

So Jesus explained himself at length. "I'm telling you this straight. The Son can't independently do a thing, only what he sees the Father doing. What the Father does, the Son does. The Father loves the Son and includes him in everything he is doing (John 5:19-20, The Message Bible). [10]

So Jesus answered them by saying, "I assure you and most solemnly say to you, the Son can do nothing of Himself [of His own accord], unless it is something He sees the Father doing; for whatever things the Father does, the Son [in His turn] also does in the same way. For the Father dearly loves the Son and shows Him everything that He Himself is doing; and the Father will show Him greater works than these, so that you will be filled with wonder" (John 5:19-20, Amplified Bible).

---

[10] Please note the present ongoing tense of this verse "is doing." The present, ongoing tense is found in most translations. This indicates there is no end to what the Father is doing in the world, and through the Church as we follow the teachings, demonstrations, and precepts that Jesus taught from the Father. Bold type is used to highlight the part under discussion.

Now that some background has been laid, we will move forward to what Jesus said about the Kingdom of God/Heaven in the four gospel accounts. As we consider what the Kingdom of God/heaven is that Jesus taught, we need to ask ourselves these questions: "Do I believe it as taught in the Bible, or am I trying to fit the Bible into my paradigm of a particular church tradition instead of taking it at face value? Am I asking the Holy Spirit to guide my understanding, or am I depending on what someone else has told me?" When we ask the Holy Spirit to lead and guide us as we study God's Word, I can promise you may well have your theological viewpoint turned upside down or at least enhanced to do as Jesus did.

Chapter 6:

Worship the King

This chapter will continue to lay additional groundwork on who Jesus is and where his authority comes from. To begin, I will explore why God has a kingdom, who lives in it, the kingdom's rules, and how to be successful in it.

First of all, we need to review the story of the wise men and their visit to Bethlehem. Have you ever thought why they went straight to Herod's palace to inquire of him where the newborn king could be found? Why didn't they just ask someone on the edge of town or in the middle of the town as they came into town?

At this point, I think it will be helpful to provide some background information on these wise men who came from the East because they saw a star unlike any other they had ever seen before.

Who were these 'wise men'? Only Matthew records their visit in twelve short verses. Contrary to popular Christmas tradition, the

Bible does not use the terms "three wise men" or "three kings" to describe the travelers from the East who visited Jesus offering gifts of gold, frankincense, and myrrh. Instead, the Gospel writer Matthew used the Greek word magos to describe those who visited Jesus. This word was first used for members of a caste of priests and wise men among the Medes, Persians, and Babylonians, whose learning was chiefly astronomy, astrology, and enchantment.

We first see the use of the word magoi (plural) or magos (singular) in the Greek translation of the Old Testament called the Septuagint, as used in the book of Daniel. For example, Daniel 5:11 says that Daniel was made *"chief of the magicians, enchanters, Chaldeans, and astrologers."* In other words, he was made chief of this group of learned, wise men.

If you recall, Daniel was taken captive to Babylon, where he was used by King Nebuchadnezzar to interpret dreams. Also, another king of Babylon, Belshazzar, *"summoned the enchanters, astrologers, and diviners"* to tell him what the writing on the wall meant, but they couldn't, so Daniel was called, and he was able to explain it to the king. If you recall that very night, Darius the Mede invaded the Babylonian Empire and conquered it. He made Daniel one of his administrators. Daniel also served under Cyrus, the Persian king who succeeded Darius.

Based on this history, it is often assumed that these magi who came from the East to visit Jesus were from the area of the old

Persian Empire. At its height, it encompassed the areas of modern-day Iran, Egypt, Turkey, and parts of Afghanistan and Pakistan.

Even though it seems we celebrate Jesus' birth with the shepherds present and then the "wise men," those visitors from the East were not there at Jesus' birth. Also, there were not just three magi. Eastern tradition says there were twelve magi, while Western tradition lists three magi based on the three gifts that were presented to Jesus. The three gifts were gold, which helped pay the way to go to Egypt to escape Herod's murderous plot to kill all baby boys under the age of two. Frankincense is an aromatic resin used in perfumes and incense. The word is French, and it literally means 'high-quality incense'. Myrrh was a gum resin used in incense and perfume, as well as for medicinal reasons.

These magi were probably Zoroastrian priests who were astrologers who were used to looking at the stars and reading significance into them. The question then becomes: why were these magi so taken with this bright star that they were willing to put together a large caravan and travel hundreds of miles across all kinds of rough terrain, carrying valuables that at today's prices were more than four million dollars? In fact, the frankincense and myrrh were worth more than the gold that was brought to Jesus.

I believe the answer to that must go back to the time Daniel spent as the chief of astrologers and astronomers. Daniel would have known about the prediction that the prophet Isaiah had made of a coming messiah, the son of God. I am sure that Daniel would have told of some of these prophecies from Isaiah to his fellow astrologers so they could be on the lookout for anything unusual in the heavens that might indicate something important was going to happen. There are several instances in secular history that the Greek historian Herodotus tells of events that foretold the birth of King Cyrus.

These heavenly events did not take place for the average person, but only when someone special was to be born or die, etc. So, when these magi who came to visit Jesus saw this heavenly star, they knew something of importance was being foretold. According to scripture, they went first to Jerusalem. Why? Because Jerusalem was the capital of the area that the star had directed them to. And of course, being very important people from their own country, they went to the king's palace, because that is where they expected to find a baby of royal birth. Herod really didn't know what was going on, as his family had been Jewish converts. While he may have known something of the Jewish religion and traditions, he would not have been highly educated in the finer points of Isaiah's promise of a heavenly son of God who was to come to save His people from their sins.

After finding out that there was to be a king born in Bethlehem, Herod directed the magi to that small town. The Bible says, *"After they had heard the king, they went their way, and look!*

Patricia C. Friel

The star they had seen when they were in the East went ahead of them until it came to stop above where the young child was. (Matthew 2:9). Matthew 2:11 tells us that *"When they went into the house, they saw the young child with Mary his mother."* There was no newborn baby in a stable that the magi visited. This could easily have been a child up to a year or maybe even slightly older. We know that Herod had spent some time quizzing the magi when they came to ask *"where the one born King of the Jews"* was. Herod had a timeline, and so when he ordered the death of all baby boys, he kept it under the age of two.

At this point, some of you may ask how the story of the magi fits into a discussion on the Kingdom of God/heaven. I wanted to lay the groundwork that shows Jesus came as a king, was recognized as such by other important kings, and was worshipped as such. His coming had been prophesied by Isaiah.

I want to emphasize that we are children of a king and live in a king's kingdom. As such, we have certain rights and responsibilities and can expect certain things from our king as we obey His principles and precepts.

All of this started when the Godhead (Father, Son, and Holy Spirit) said,

Let us make man in Our image, according to Our likeness, so that they may rule over the fish in the sea and the birds in the sky, over the livestock and all the wild animals, and over all the

creatures that move along the ground...And God blessed them and said to them, "Be fruitful and increase in number; fill the earth and subdue it. Rule over the fish in the sea and the birds in the sky and over every living creature that moves on the ground. (Genesis 1:26-28)

As you can see, God gave humankind the command to rule over the kingdom of this earth. Only kings can give kingdoms and award rulership to people. As we know, man rebelled against God and decided to do things his way. This rebellion was labeled sin in God's sight. In other words, mankind mounted an insurrection against the Kingdom of God. God put up with mankind for centuries, trying to get their attention and bring them back into compliance with His kingdom principles. He sent a flood, He caused the languages to become differentiated from one another at the Tower of Babel, He finally said that all of humankind was impossible to deal with, so He chose a man, Abraham, and began to deal with just one family. Try as hard as he might, even Abraham could not get things entirely right, as seen by his fathering two boys, Ishmael and Isaac, who even now continue to fight among themselves. The rest of the Old Testament is the story of God's dealings with humankind, their sins, and the judgments that occurred because of their sins.

Finally, God chose to send His son, Jesus, the Messiah, to earth to teach people, on an individual basis, how to live in His kingdom. God's whole compassionate giving of His son can be summed up in John 3:16-21:

For God so loved the world that He gave His only begotten Son that whoever believes in him should not perish but have eternal life. For God did not send His Son into the world to condemn the world, but to save the world through him. Whoever believes in him is not condemned, but whoever does not believe stands condemned already because they have not believed in the name of God's one and only Son. This is the verdict: Light has come into the world, but people loved darkness instead of light because their deeds were evil. Everyone who does evil hates the light and will not come into the light for fear that their deeds will be exposed. But whoever lives by the truth comes into the light, so that it may be seen plainly that what they have done has been done in the sight of God.

Now it is up to each person, on an individual basis, to respond to Jesus' love and his ability to show us how to live a kingdom life that is pleasing to God the Father. We will continue to look at what Jesus has to say about how the Kingdom of God works. As children of the king, we need to know how to live in God's kingdom.

Ask yourself if you are ready for the challenge. It may cause you to shift how you view yourself in relation to the Father and His call on your life and ministry. I want to add, at this point, that the church has elevated certain people as having a specific call on their lives to do ministry. Yet, Jesus calls everyone to share and participate in the ministry of the Kingdom of God. The book of Acts proves that not just the apostles but also many, who are considered lay people of the church, turned their communities upside down because they had the boldness to share the Kingdom of God with their friends and neighbors.[11]

In the church today, we have relegated certain people with titles to share Jesus with others. Yes, some people have been called by God to fulfill certain positions that we honor in the body. But that does not mean that everyone else can stand back and let them do the work of carrying the Kingdom of God to the hurting, needy people we encounter in the marketplace, the workplace, school, and yes, even church. It was not just the eleven apostles in the upper room in the book of Acts that received the Holy Spirit. There were 120 men and women present that day. Peter might have preached the sermon that saw 5000 people being saved. But it took everyone to nurture, teach, and care for them. No one gets off easy in the Kingdom of God. We are all called to tasks in God's kingdom on earth.

---

[11] Acts 6-7 The story of Stephen. Acts 8:4- 8; 26-40 The story of Philip. Acts 9:36-40 The story of Dorcas. Acts 10:22-24 The story of Cornelius. Acts 11:19-21 The church in Antioch. Romans 16 lists the various house churches and the people who may have been their leaders or at least showed hospitality for the gatherings.

Chapter 7:

The Kingly Message

To start, I want to give you some facts about the Kingdom of God/Heaven found in the New Testament. When the term "Kingdom of God" is used, Mark uses it 14 times, and Luke uses it 32 times. The synonymous phrase "Kingdom of Heaven" appears 32 times in the Gospel of Matthew alone. Altogether, the phrase Kingdom of God is used 62 times throughout the Gospels, Acts, Romans, 1 Corinthians, Galatians, Colossians, and 2 Thessalonians. In the New Testament Gospels, Jesus is almost always speaking of the Kingdom, the Kingdom of God, or the Kingdom of Heaven, in some way. Many of his parables explain something about this Kingdom: *"It is like a mustard seed. It is like a treasure. It is like a merchant looking for pearls. It is like a king who prepared a wedding banquet for his son."* In Luke 4:43, Jesus defines the purpose of his coming in light of the Kingdom: *"I must*

proclaim the good news of the Kingdom of God to the other cities also; for I was sent for this purpose."

Considering the centrality of Jesus' teachings on the Kingdom of God and his actions while walking on this earth, it is strange that many Christians are relatively unfamiliar with what this phrase actually means. However, if we want to understand the whole message of Jesus, that is, his preaching, teaching, ministry of healings, miracles, and deliverance, as well as his death and resurrection, it is necessary to understand what he meant when he spoke of the Kingdom of God/Kingdom of heaven.

Gordon Fee, a theologian, Biblical commentator, and seminary professor of New Testament, once said in a lecture on Jesus, "You cannot know anything about Jesus, I repeat, anything, if you miss the Kingdom of God…You are zero on Jesus if you don't understand this term. I'm sorry to say it that strongly, but this is the great failure of evangelical Christianity. We have had Jesus without the Kingdom of God, and therefore have literally done Jesus in."[12]

I want to backtrack for a few minutes. If you were to ask the average person on the street, or even Christians sitting in a church pew, what Jesus' most important message was, they would all say,

---

[12] Gordon Fee, "Jesus: Early Ministry/Kingdom of God," lecture delivered at Regent College, Tape Series 2235E, Pt.1. Copyright © Regent College, Vancouver, B.C., Canada.

"something about love." Some people might even remember that Jesus called his followers to love their enemies. Jesus did talk quite a bit about love. In fact, in John 13:34, he told the disciples this, *"A new command I give you: Love one another."* He repeats it in John 15:12 and 17. Jesus even said it in Mark 12:29-31, *"Love the Lord, your God with all your heart and with all your soul and with all your mind and with all your strength. The second is this: "Love your neighbor as yourself. There is no commandment greater than these."*

Yet, love was not the core of what Jesus taught. Think about this: if Jesus had been running around first-century Judea, Galilee, Samaria, and Jerusalem telling people to love each other, he certainly would not have been tortured and hanged on a cross to die. Something else to think about, who cares if someone tells you to love someone you naturally hate, like the Jews hated the Romans? They would have dismissed Jesus. And the Romans, the obvious enemies of these first-century Jews, wouldn't have crucified someone whose main message was telling the Jews to love them and turn the other cheek. If anything, the Romans would probably have protected Jesus as a peacemaker. So, when you think about it, the core of his message to the people of his day must have been much more contentious than just calling people to love one another and turn the other cheek.

What Jesus taught, preached, and demonstrated really got people riled up. It even got the demons riled up. And of course, the Jewish religious leaders and teachers of the Temple were absolutely livid the majority of the time whenever Jesus was around, healing people, performing miracles, and delivering people from demons.

Mark 1:15 summarizes the core of Jesus's teaching: *"The time is fulfilled, and the Kingdom of God has come near. Repent, and believe in the good news."*

Different religious traditions have equated this saying of Jesus to many different interpretations. Some have claimed that it is heaven, and that Jesus was saying, in so many words, "Now you can go to heaven when you die." Others have understood "the Kingdom of God" as referring to the Church. From their perspective, Jesus announced the beginning of the age of the Church versus Temple worship. Still others have seen the Kingdom of God as a world infused by divine justice. They have used this scripture as a call to social action. Others have reduced the Kingdom of God to inner awareness of one's own divinity, meaning they see themselves as divine beings while living on earth.

However, all of these fail to take seriously both what Jesus actually says about the Kingdom of God and what his fellow Jews, especially the Old Testament prophets, had been speaking about the kingdom for centuries.

The problem with trying to understand what Jesus meant by the Kingdom of God and how we understand it is a language issue. In everyday English, "kingdom" means a place where a king reigns. The kingdom of Great Britain, where King Charles reigns, is a specific place – the British Isles. But when Jesus spoke of the Kingdom of God, he did not think in terms of locality, but of authority.

In the New Testament Gospels, Jesus uses the Greek phrase *he basileia tou theou*, "the Kingdom of God." The word *basileia* could sometimes refer to a locale over which a king ruled, but its primary meaning in the first century was "reign, rule, authority, sovereignty." The same is true of the Aramaic term, *malku*, the word which was probably spoken by Jesus. We can see this meaning clearly in one of Jesus' parables. Luke 19:12 describes a nobleman who *"went to a distant country to have himself appointed king and then to return."* The NRSV reads it this way, *"to get royal power for himself."* The Greek of this verse reads literally, *"he went to a distant country to receive a basileia for himself."* This king did not go to get a new region over which to rule, but rather to get new and greater authority over the place where he already lived.

This same meaning of kingdom can be found in Hebrew in Psalm 145:10-11, where we read: *"All your works shall give thanks to you, O LORD, and all your faithful shall bless you. They shall speak of the glory of your kingdom (malkuth in Hebrew; basileia in Greek) and tell of your power."*

Here, God's kingdom is parallel to divine power, not to the place over which God reigns. God's faithful praise God's sovereignty here, not the place over which God is sovereign.

So, when Jesus proclaims that the Kingdom of God has come near, he doesn't mean that a place is approaching, but that God's own royal authority and power have come on the scene. Therefore, we can paraphrase Mark 1:15, which summarizes Jesus' preaching, as follows: *"God's reign is at hand. God's power is being unleashed. Turn your life around and put your trust in this good news."*[13]

Of course, Jesus' announcement of God's reign did not come in a vacuum. It was both consistent with and a fulfillment of a central theme in the Hebrew prophets, especially parts of Isaiah.

The next chapter will continue to explore what living in the Kingdom of God means for us as followers of Christ Jesus. Here

---

[13] "The [appointed period of] time is fulfilled, and the kingdom of God is at hand; repent [change your inner self – your old way of thinking, regret past sins, live your life in a way that proves repentance; seek God's purpose for your life] and believe [with a deep, abiding trust] in the good news [regarding salvation]." (Amplified Bible for Mark 1:15).

Patricia C. Friel

are some scriptures from both the Old Testament and New Testament to read and reflect upon to enhance our understanding of Jesus' mission and how it impacts believers today:

- Zephaniah 3:14-20
- Isaiah 52:7-10
- Ezekiel 17:22-23
- Mark 4:30-32

Chapter 8:
Here And Now

So far, we have established that Jesus is king and that people came to worship him like a king, even at his birth. We then looked at the many times Jesus made reference to the Kingdom of God or the kingdom of heaven as he went about teaching and preaching. The key verse to remember is Mark 1:15, *"The time is fulfilled, and the Kingdom of God has come near; repent, and believe in the good news."*

We also learned that the word "kingdom" in the phrase "Kingdom of God" misses the precise sense of Jesus' own language. What he proclaimed was not the approach of a place where God rules, but rather the dawning of God's kingly authority on earth. Therefore, when we read or hear the phrase "Kingdom of God" in the Gospels, we need to think in terms of God's reign, rule, authority, or sovereignty. This is what Jesus was announcing when he said, *"...the Kingdom of God has come near..."*

Patricia C. Friel

Remember, Jesus spoke to the Jewish people of the land of Israel. They knew the scriptures that promised them hope from oppressors. They knew the scriptures which promised that He would come and rule over them. In the Jewish mindset, they were looking for an earthly king who would come and set them free from Roman oppression. They were looking for a king who had a specific piece of land to rule over. Yet, the prophets spoke in terms of God's kingdom where the Lord would rule over his people, not a piece of land.

In the last chapter, I suggested that you might want to read Zephaniah 3:14-20 and Isaiah 52:7-10. In those two passages, we have God stating that at the right time, the LORD himself will be the 'king of Israel.' It is in that role that God's people will have victory, remove their oppressors, gather their scattered exiles, and restore their fortunes. Also, there is a promise of peace, the return of the LORD to Jerusalem, joyful singing, comfort, and redemption for Judah, and the impact of God's salvation upon the whole earth. The announcement of God's reign would, of course, be good news. This is why Jesus declared, *"The time is fulfilled, and the Kingdom of God has come near; repent and believe in the good news."* Of course, the prophets were looking ahead to an undetermined time in the future when God would return to rule, but Jesus says, *"The time is now. The reign of God has now come near. So, turn your life around and live in light of this truth."*

I want to move forward now that I've established that Jesus' central message was, "The Kingdom of God has come near," to show that it was the reign of God he was talking about. It was the reign of God—God's rule, authority, and power—that Jesus was saying was at hand, not a particular piece of land.

At times, such as in Mark 1:15, Jesus simply and bluntly states that the presence of the kingdom is now here. However, Jesus goes on to explain and demonstrate this kingdom, and that is what we will look at now.

In Mark 10:14-15, he says, *"Let the little children come to me; do not stop them; for it is to such as these that the Kingdom of God belongs. Truly I tell you, whoever does not receive the Kingdom of God as a little child will never enter it."* Jesus' point, that one must receive the kingdom in a childlike manner, provides some more information about God's kingdom.

The Kingdom of God is not something we create by our own efforts, but rather something we receive. Have you ever heard Christians saying things like, "It is our duty to bring in the kingdom" or "Our vision is to usher in God's kingdom." This misses the point that Jesus was trying to make entirely. He is saying that God inaugurated God's own reign. Whatever our relationship is to the kingdom, we don't initiate it, produce it, bring it in, or inaugurate it. This is God's domain, and He does all the work. All we need to do is believe it and accept it as He instructs us.

I want to provide some scripture that we call parables, which Jesus used to explain the Kingdom of God. Some of his parables have examples from the Old Testament. Mark 4:30-32 says,

With what can we compare the Kingdom of God, or what parable will we use for it? It is like a mustard seed, which, when sown upon the ground, is the smallest of all the seeds on earth; yet when it is sown, it grows up and becomes the greatest of all shrubs, and puts forth large branches, so that the birds of the air can make nests in its shade.

Now consider what the prophet Ezekiel wrote in 17:22-23,

I myself will take a sprig from the lofty top of a cedar; I will set it out. I will break off a tender one from the topmost of its young twigs; I myself will plant it on a high and lofty mountain. On the mountain height of Israel I will plant it, in order that it may produce boughs and bear fruit, and become a noble cedar. Under it, every kind of bird will live; in the shade of its branches will nest winged creatures of every kind.

As you can see, Jesus reveals that the reign of God, which the Jews expected to come in like a thundering herd, will begin small and insignificant, but will grow and expand and become exceptionally large in size compared to how it began. Whereas Ezekiel spoke of a tiny cedar sprig that grew into a noble cedar in which birds would nest. Jesus used the same imagery to make a point about God's kingdom. Though Jesus' ministry began humbly, with just himself and then the twelve men he chose to spend time with, along with some other men and women, with whom he interacted on occasion, it has grown into a worldwide movement that attracts people of all nations. Eventually, God's kingdom will become the final rule of all that is His to reign.

Returning to what I said earlier: God initiated His own reign, and it is not our responsibility or duty to bring it in. Jesus started with a few disciples. By the time he ascended into heaven, as recorded in the first chapter of Acts, there were 120 who gathered daily to pray and wait on the coming of the Holy Spirit, which Jesus had promised. After the Holy Spirit descended, people began gathering around the house where the disciples had been praying together, in one accord. The coming of the Holy Spirit was not a quiet action but one that got people's attention. Then, when Peter stood up to explain what was happening, Acts 2:41 tells us, *"Those who accepted his message were baptized, and about three thousand were added to their number that day."* This was all the work of God, not man, for that exponential growth in a matter of hours. We proclaim, and God gives the increase in His kingdom.

Remember, Mark 1:15, *"…the Kingdom of God has come near; repent, and believe in the good news."* That was the message Peter gave to the people gathered outside the upper room that day when they asked in response to the scripture Peter shared with them about who Jesus was. He said to them, *"Repent and be baptized, every one of you, in the name of Jesus Christ for the forgiveness of your sins. And you will receive the gift of the Holy Spirit. The promise is for you and your children and for all who are far off – for all whom the Lord our God will call."*

As you can see, this is God's kingdom, God's reign, and God is the initiator of all that is within His kingdom. We are only His hands extended. He gives the increase. We just follow His instructions and reap His promises to increase His kingdom.

I digress. Let me say that we have seen thus far how Jesus announces the presence of God's reign through basic statements, explanations, and parables. As important as his words were, they do not exhaust the only way that he proclaimed that the Kingdom of God was in the midst of those people he encountered daily, nor even in our midst today. Jesus also engaged in works that revealed the presence of the kingdom. His works took various forms, such as healings, exorcisms, nature miracles, and other symbolic gestures that I will explain later.

I want to close this chapter by providing you with some scriptures to read that will enhance your learning curve as we continue with the various ways that Jesus exhibited that the

'Kingdom of God' was in the midst of people whenever he was around. [14]

---

[14] Mark 4:30-32, 10:14-15; Isaiah 53:7-10

Chapter 9:

Teaching Plus Demonstration

Remember, Jesus spoke to the Jewish people of the land of Israel. They knew the scriptures that promised them hope from oppressors. They knew the scriptures which promised that He would come and rule over them. In the Jewish mindset, they were looking for an earthly king who would come and set them free from Roman oppression. They were looking for a king who had a specific piece of land to rule over. Yet, the prophets spoke in terms of God's kingdom where the Lord would rule over his people, not a piece of land.

Now we are going to explore what Jesus said about himself in Luke 4:18-19, as he stood up in the synagogue and read from Isaiah 61:1-2.

The Spirit of the Lord is upon me, because he has anointed me to proclaim good news to the poor. He has sent me to proclaim freedom for the prisoners and recovery of sight for the blind, to set the oppressed free, to proclaim the year of the Lord's favor.

If you continue to read the passage in Luke, Jesus sat down after reading the scripture and then told the people in the synagogue, *"Today this scripture is fulfilled in your midst."* After some more conversation with the people assembled in the synagogue, the result was that the people became so "furious" that they got up and drove Jesus out of town, tried to throw him over a hill to his death, but scripture records that he *"walked right through the crowd and went on his way."*

As can be seen, mere words alone were not enough to convince the people that he was the Son of God. However, the rest of Jesus' ministry is comprised of words plus works. The words spoke of the Kingdom of God, and the works Jesus did demonstrated the Presence of the Kingdom in the midst of the people. It was necessary to have a combination of both words and works. Words alone are cheap. However, when Jesus demonstrated the power of God and how His kingdom operated, it grabbed people's attention. They were willing to listen to the parables because they saw the works for themselves. They were hurting people, both physically, spiritually, and emotionally – just like everyone today. People have not changed. Their needs have not changed.

Based on the Luke/Isaiah passages, we will look at how Jesus demonstrated that God's kingdom was at hand. Jesus engaged in healing people of various diseases. He performed exorcisms, he demonstrated the power of God over nature, and he performed other demonstrative gestures. I want to share something about each one of the ways that Jesus demonstrated that the Kingdom of God operated in the lives of the people that Jesus encountered. As I do, I want you to remember Malachi 3:6 states, *"I the LORD do not change."* And Hebrews 13:8 says, *"Jesus Christ is the same yesterday and today and forever."* All that Jesus taught and demonstrated has not changed.

People have tried to say that Jesus' teachings and demonstrations of power are irrelevant to today's world. If you recall, Eve told God she was deceived by the serpent, but Adam was not deceived. He acted in willful disobedience to God's instruction not to eat of the tree in the middle of the garden.

Today, God's Word provides a *"Light unto our feet and lamp unto our path"* (Psalm 119:105). Everything that Jesus taught and demonstrated is relevant today, without question, just as it was in his day. So, as we look at how Jesus demonstrated how the Kingdom of God is to operate on earth, let us keep in mind that *"God is the same yesterday, today, and forever."* He does not change. We think that because we live in a modern age, where science can explain everything, we do not need to follow the pattern laid out by Jesus. In our own way, we are just as disobedient as Adam was in the Garden.

As we consider all the demonstrations of the kingdom's power, remember that in the Old Testament, many of these demonstrations were also present through the lives of the prophets of God, just not on the same level as demonstrated through Jesus. They were rarer, but still present. The prophets of old were operating only as the Spirit of God would come upon them. Jesus operated because, according to all the gospel accounts of the baptism of Jesus by John the Baptist, the Spirit of God came upon Jesus at the beginning of his ministry, and God proclaimed from the heavens, *"You are my Son, whom I love; with you I am well pleased."* Scripture goes on to say that *"Jesus was full of the Holy Spirit..."*

As we explore all that Jesus did, we must remember that he was teaching those around him how to operate in God's kingdom on earth. John 14:12-13 says,

Very truly I tell you, whoever believes in me will do the works I have been doing, and they will do even greater things than these, because I am going to the Father. And I will do whatever you ask in my name, so that the Father may be glorified in the Son. You may ask me for anything in my name, and I will do it.

Patricia C. Friel

Jesus placed one caveat on his followers just before he ascended into heaven. Acts 1:4b-5,8 tells us that Jesus told his followers who were gathered in the upper room (all 120 of them):

Do not leave Jerusalem, but wait for the gift my Father promised, which you have heard me speak about. For John baptized with water, but in a few days you will be baptized with the Holy Spirit...But you will receive power when the Holy Spirit comes on you, and you will be my witnesses...

Jesus' ministry of the Kingdom of God, present on earth, began after his baptism by the Holy Spirit. It included healings, exorcisms, nature miracles, and other symbolic gestures. As far as healings went, Isaiah 35:5-6 proclaimed ahead of time that the presence of God's reign on earth would include salvation and redemption for His people. In that context, we read this promise,

Then the eyes of the blind shall be opened, and the ears of the deaf unstopped; then the lame shall leap like a deer, and the tongue of the speechless sing for joy.

When John the Baptist's disciples came to Jesus to ask, on John's behalf, if Jesus was the one promised who would bring in the Kingdom of God, Jesus' response was, *"Go and tell John what you hear and see; the blind receive their sight, the lame walk, the lepers are cleansed, the deaf hear, the dead are raised, and the poor have good news brought to them"* (Matthew 11:4-5). Jesus was saying to John's disciples that the promise of Isaiah 35:5-6 was happening in his ministry and that, yes, he was the one through whom God's kingdom had come.

Interestingly enough, as soon as Jesus left the synagogue in Nazareth, after reading Isaiah 61:1-2, he went to Capernaum, a town in Galilee, and was teaching in the synagogue there on a Sabbath day. During his teaching, Luke 4:33-36 tells us,

In the synagogue, there was a man possessed by a demon, an impure spirit. He cried out at the top of his voice, 'Go away! What do you want with us, Jesus of Nazareth? Have you come to destroy us? I know who you are – the Holy One of God!' Be quiet! Jesus said sternly. "Come out of him!" Then the demon threw the man down before them all and came out without injuring him. All the people were amazed and said to each other, "What words these are! With authority and power, he gives orders to impure spirits, and they are coming out!

Many people do not believe that people can have demons, especially in America. However, there is no debate in other countries, such as in the Southern Hemisphere and on the African continent. Whether you believe people in the Northern hemisphere can be influenced by demons who cause them to do evil things or not, exorcisms were central to Jesus' ministry during his time on earth. There is also a record of the disciples in the book of Acts exercising authority over people who had demons. But as to Jesus and the people of his day, when some of the Pharisees accused

Jesus of casting out demons with demonic power, he answered them by declaring,

Every kingdom divided against itself will be ruined, and every city or household divided against itself will not stand. If Satan drives out Satan, he is divided against himself. How then can his kingdom stand? And if I drive out demons by Beelzebul, by whom do your people drive them out? So then, they will be your judges. But if it is by the Spirit of God that I drive out demons, then the Kingdom of God has come upon you (Matthew 12:25-28).

For Jesus and the first-century Jews, being able to cast out demons was a demonstration of the Presence of God in their midst and His kingdom. It was also a demonstration of the superiority of God over all other gods.

The nature miracles of Jesus, according to the Gospels, include multiplying food to feed masses of people.[15] He walks on the water and even commands Peter to walk on the water. He spoke to the storm that threatened to overturn the boat, and said, *"Peace, be still!"* The storm immediately subsided. Psalm 89:8-9 states, *"O LORD God of hosts, who is as mighty as you, O LORD? Your faithfulness surrounds you. You rule the raging of the sea; when its waves rise, you still them."* This suggests that God's promised

---

[15] See an Old Testament reference to multiplying food in 2 Kings 4:42-44.

kingdom has arrived and that God himself is present in the ministry of Jesus.

It is the works of Jesus that give credence to the message that he has come to bring the Kingdom of God to earth. The gospel writers interweave Jesus' miracles with his message, and all is based on Old Testament writings that Jesus proclaimed from Isaiah 61:1-2.[16]

Some other prophetic acts that Jesus did to help his hearers take his pronouncement that the Kingdom of God was among them were: He ate with social and religious outcasts—sinners by the religious leaders of the day's designation. This showed God's inclusiveness in His reign on earth. All who come to Him with a repentant heart shall see the Kingdom of God on earth, as in heaven. Jesus also welcomed little children, and said of them, *"Let the little children come to me; do not stop them, for it is to such as these that the Kingdom of God belongs"* (Mark 10:14). In other words, let us live joyfully and believe all that Jesus said and taught. Also, in this statement is the concept of being totally dependent upon the Father. Children had to be totally dependent upon their earthly fathers to provide all their needs. Jesus wants his disciples

---

[16] The Spirit of the Sovereign LORD is on me, because the LORD has anointed me to proclaim good news to the poor. He has sent me to bind up the brokenhearted, to proclaim freedom for the captives and release from darkness for the prisoners, to proclaim the year of the LORD'S favor and the day of vengeance of our God, to comfort all who mourn…"

to understand they need to be totally dependent upon him and not make decisions that do not include his Father's will or direction, just as he is totally dependent upon God to lead, guide, and direct.

Chapter 10:
The Kingdom of God

*"T*he Spirit of the Lord is upon me, because he has anointed me to proclaim good news to the poor. He has sent me to proclaim freedom to prisoners and recovery of sight to the blind, to set the oppressed free, to proclaim the year of the Lord's favor."* If you recall, the people became incensed at his words and tried to throw him off a cliff in his hometown. We learned that words alone would not change people's minds, so Jesus demonstrated God's power over physical ailments and conditions, and emotional and spiritual problems. He healed the deaf, blind, and lame, drove out demons, and raised the dead, and people's spiritual eyes were opened at his teaching concerning the Law of Moses when He said in Matthew 15:18-20 and in a parallel passage in Mark 7:20:

But the things that come out of a person's mouth come from the heart, and these defile them. For out of the heart come evil thoughts – murder, adultery, sexual immorality, theft, false testimony, slander. These are what defile a person, but eating with unwashed hands does not defile.

What comes out of a person is what defiles them. For it is from within, out of a person's heart, that evil thoughts come – sexual immorality, theft, murder, adultery, greed, malice, deceit, lewdness, envy, slander, arrogance, and folly.

We also learned that because of Jesus' life, death, resurrection, and his instructions to the new church that was meeting in the Upper Room, upon his return to his Father, he would send the Holy Spirit to *"baptize them with power and as a result of being baptized with the Holy Spirit they were to become his witnesses in Jerusalem, and in all Judea and Samaria, and to the ends of the earth."* Some of Jesus' parting thoughts to his disciples on the night he was betrayed and arrested are found in John 14:11-12:

Believe me when I say that I am in the Father and the Father is in me; or at least believe on the evidence of the works themselves. Very truly I tell you, whoever believes in me will do the works I have been doing, and they will do even greater things than these, because I am going to the Father.

If I were to go out on the street, or even into churches, and ask the question, "Where is the Kingdom of God today?" I am sure the majority of the answers I would receive would be something like, "In my heart," or "Up in heaven." If that were your answer, then I have to say we are limiting the dimensions of the reality of who God is and the authority He gave to His son, who passed God's Kingdom authority on to us who believe. Remember, God's Kingdom is not land or a certain territory. It is where His authority, rule, dominion, and reign dominate. In other words, God has ALL power, ALL authority, and reigns over ALL His creation and humankind. In Ephesians 1:18-23, Paul puts it very clearly,

…that the eyes of your heart may be enlightened in order that you may know the hope to which he has called you, the riches of his glorious inheritance in his holy people, and his incomparably great power for us who believe. That power is the same as the mighty strength he exerted when he raised Christ from the dead and seated him at his right hand in the heavenly realms, far above all rule and authority, power and dominion, and every name that is invoked, not only in the present age but also in the one to come. And God placed all things under his feet and appointed him to be head over everything for the church, which is his body, the fullness of him who fills everything in every way.

Because of who Jesus is in God and who we are in Jesus, the reign of God touches every dimension of reality throughout the whole earth. God's rules and precepts should, but of course they do not, impact our actions and relationships with one another, our thoughts, our government, our heart relationship with Jesus, and how we believe who we are in Christ Jesus. If we understand who we are in Christ Jesus, then we too can say our ministry includes, *"The Spirit of the Lord is upon me, because he has anointed me to proclaim good news to the poor. He has sent me to proclaim freedom to prisoners and recovery of sight to the blind, to set the oppressed free, to proclaim the year of the Lord's favor."* That means we should be experiencing all that Jesus demonstrated to his disciples, so they too could minister to whoever they met in power and authority, over physical and soul sicknesses, leading people to Christ, thus healing spiritual sickness and feelings of being lost and hopeless. Through Jesus Christ, we are the carriers of the light and the hope to the lost, wherever we meet them. Therefore, the Kingdom of God is within us, should we choose to believe that he lives and will fulfill all of his promises to his followers.

Did Jesus bring all of God's kingdom to earth? The answer is both YES and NO. Can we bring all of God's kingdom to others on earth? The answer is both YES and NO! I will give you an example. When I was completing my doctorate, I did two and a half years of research and writing. Then, in the last semester, I had to meet with a committee of seven people and defend what I had researched and written. After responding to their questions and listening to their comments, I had to leave the room while they discussed all they had read and heard. (Talk about a fluttering heart!) After about 15 minutes, they called me back in. They all had big smiles and said, "Congratulations, Dr. Friel." Was I really Dr. Friel at that point? Not really. I had not yet walked down the aisle or received my diploma signed by the head of the doctoral program, the board of regents, or the seminary president. So, it is like the Kingdom of God, it is the already, but not yet, kingdom. It is here, but not yet fully realized. We can be about the Father's business, doing what Jesus taught and commanded, but the fullness of the Kingdom will not be totally present until the end of time. Revelation 21:1-8 records it like this,

Then I saw "a new heaven and a new earth, for the first heaven and the first earth had passed away, and there was no longer any sea. I saw the Holy City, the new Jerusalem, coming down out of heaven from God, prepared as a bride beautifully dressed for her husband. And I heard a loud voice from the throne saying, "Look! God's dwelling place is now among the people, and God himself will be with them and be their God. He will wipe every tear from their eyes. There will be no more death or mourning or crying or pain, for the old order of things has passed away. He who was seated on the throne said, "I am making everything new." Then he said, "Write this down, for these words are trustworthy and true." He said to me, "It is done. I am the Alpha and the Omega, the Beginning and the End. To the thirsty I will give water without cost from the spring of the water of life. Those who are victorious will inherit all this, and I will be their God, and they will be my children. But the cowardly, the unbelieving, the vile, the murderers, the sexually immoral, those who practice magic arts, the idolaters, and all liars – they will be consigned to the fiery lake of burning sulfur. This is the second death.

As you can see, the Kingdom of God, thanks to Jesus' willingness to become the sacrificial lamb for the forgiveness of our sins, is now among us in power, grace, love, and compassion for healing, deliverance, and salvation. But the fullness of God's Kingdom is yet to come at the end of time. But with the anointing of the Holy Spirit, which Jesus promised, we can be carriers of the Kingdom of God on this earth to all we meet. Just like my being addressed as Doctor Friel at the close of my defense, I was a doctor of the church, but not yet fully enjoying all the benefits of that title until I actually held my signed diploma in my hands.

All of us, who are called by the name of Jesus, can be carriers of the Kingdom of God and enjoy being able to pass on the benefits of the Kingdom. Just like in all of history, there are people who are lost, who are seeking, who are sick, and who are impacted by the present evil in the world. They need Jesus in all of his power to set them free. He has passed this task on to the Church to carry out his mission. As followers of Jesus, we should be doing the works of Jesus. As in the days of the apostles, the local newspapers should be able to report that a particular person was raised from the dead, healed of an incurable disease, and delivered from the power of demonic influence. We cannot wave our hands and see one hundred percent healing for everyone in this age. But we can demonstrate God's power millions of times more than we do. Still, total healing and deliverance will not be ours or anyone else's for all time, until we shall see Jesus in his full glory and experience the new heaven and the new earth. Then truly the reign of God is complete. Satan and his demon posse will be no more. No more sickness or death, or any other negative thing. We will once again be able to experience a total relationship with God as in the Garden of Eden before the fall. The challenge is, why are we waiting for Jesus' return instead of being about our Master's business and demonstrating his kingdom to the world, so that some may be saved and set free?

The problem with the Church today is that many have watered down Jesus' *command in Matthew 28:18-20:*

All authority in heaven and on earth has been given to me. Therefore, go and make disciples of all nations, baptizing them in the name of the Father and of the Son and of the Holy Spirit, and teaching them to obey everything I have commanded you. And surely I am with you always, to the very end of the age.

The teachers, pastors, evangelists, and church leaders have not heeded all that Jesus taught and demonstrated, or else, out of fear, misunderstanding, disobedience, or hardheartedness, have not carried out his mandate. They are not afraid to preach and teach that we need Jesus to forgive our sins, but they do not teach, preach, or demonstrate how to set people truly free in their souls, spirits, and physical lives. In a way, many in the Church are no different from the Pharisees and the Teachers of the Law in Jesus' day. Paul writes to Timothy, *"People will be lovers of themselves.... lovers of pleasure rather than lovers of God – having a form of godliness but denying its power. Have nothing to do with such people"* (2 Timothy 3:2-5). Are the majority of the Church and its practices and teachings any different from the Temple leaders of Jesus' day?

Chapter 11:
Abundant Life

Jesus, the Son of God, a representative from heaven to earth, was our teacher to demonstrate and train up additional sons and daughters in the ways of the Kingdom of God. He was so effective that masses of people followed him; the religious leaders of the day, for the most part, hated him. They considered Jesus a threat to their traditions and teachings. They could not fathom that God cared enough to come to earth, as a human man, to let a lost and hurting world know how to come to Him for shalom – the kind of peace that enriched the whole fabric of their lives. It would no longer be about ritual and religious practices but about the relationship between God and His created ones. No longer would there have to be an earthly priest who would be responsible for interceding on behalf of people for the forgiveness of sins, for the healing of all wounds, and deliverance from the clutches of Satan.

Patricia C. Friel

Jesus came to minister in integrity, truth, love, and compassion. He did not have an agenda of appeasement toward a foreign government; he did not love money or possessions. His was a love of a son for his Father and carrying out His instructions on how to restore people in relationship to Him and how to live an abundant kingdom life while inhabiting this earth. Jesus said in John 10:10, *"The thief comes only to steal and kill and destroy; I have come that they might have life and have it more abundantly."* This was not a promise for a future life but a promise for one's life in the here and now. How has the Church fallen so short of carrying out this promise to the hurting masses of our day?

Without meaning to, we have drifted away from the core understanding of all that Jesus intended for his followers to embrace. Jesus told people to count the cost of following him (Luke 14:25-35). It seems today that people are counting how much money they can make when they count the cost of following Jesus. This is not a new phenomenon. Throughout history, since the beginning of ecclesiastical record keeping, both Old and New Testaments speak of how the keepers of the religious practices of the day drifted from a stance of carrying out Jesus' mission of kingdom witness into practices that embraced those who had more, thus could give more, over those who had little to give. Yet, we see Jesus giving to all walks of life indiscriminately.

The church has always swung on a pendulum when it has come to following Jesus' command to *"go into all the world, preaching the gospel and baptizing in the name of the Father and of the Son and of the Holy Spirit."[17]* Generally, when people hear the call to 'leave all to follow after Jesus, the person (prophet) reminding us what the Kingdom of God requires is labeled a fanatic and made fun of, or persecuted by those who wish to live a comfortable lifestyle and still preach the gospel. God is not against wealth, power, privilege, or advancement. He is against His children making those things gods in their lives and not recognizing that He is the One who has blessed them with much so they can spread the good news of the kingdom even more. To contrast how Jesus sent people out versus how some in the church spread the gospel today is to compare traveling with nothing to arriving with jet planes and mansions.

How can we begin to change the culture of the church in our day? This is not a difficult question to answer. Instead of building edifices that speak of affluence, power, and position in a community, what would it look like if we returned to a simpler concept of church? Instead of the megachurch concept, how would

---

[17] Paul addressed some of these issues early in the life of the church. Various church fathers, as well as Martin Luther in his day, Philip Spener, John Wesley, and the Oxford Club in their day. The list can also be added from today's culture.

it be if the people of God came together in small groups to worship and care for one another? To care for the physical, emotional, economic, and spiritual needs because they are in close community with one another. To the Christians of today in our Western culture, that probably sounds scary, unattainable, and even outside of how things should be done. Yet, the house churches across cultures outside the Western world have withstood the test of time. Small gatherings allow people to watch over each other. To have the older men and women in a culture teach the younger ones how to be better parents, manage money, keep a household, mentor their spiritual growth, and gather people of all ages together to travel through the vicissitudes of life with communal support.

Of course, you may say, this sounds like the churches of Paul's day, or of John Wesley's beginning of the Methodist movement that swept America with their class bands and circuit riders. It was this type of meeting that saw the rise of the Christian faith throughout the world. It was this type of meeting that did not allow people to fall through the cracks, get discouraged, and fall from the faith. It was this type of church that held people accountable for their actions and supported them in their despondency. It was this type of church that gave immediate encouragement and guidance to all the members, children through adults. They were of one mind, in one accord, and it was easier to love one another. Everyone was family, either by genetic blood or the blood of Jesus.

Today, even in the best of churches, cliques form. So a newcomer to the fellowship feels left out and may not continue because the time to become assimilated takes too long. Yes, a church can be very intentional about welcoming the new person who may come into fellowship, but the time it takes to become part of the body, and 'in the know,' may discourage the new person. Another barrier is the way we choose to communicate with one another. Instead of having personal contact, we depend on electronic communication, which is very impersonal at best. A sense of true bonding cannot take place when people cannot see, hear, feel, and touch one another. One's true sense of self is lost to others, because it is easy to say what we think others want to hear instead of being truly seen and heard through words, unspoken body language, and facial expressions.

Jesus spent time in the presence of people. He touched them. He allowed them to touch him. In today's church culture, someone stands in front of people and teaches or preaches, and is untouchable by the viewers. It becomes a viewer culture, not an interactive culture. Even if the preacher stands at the back of the church and shakes hands as people leave, there is no opportunity for any in-depth dialogue. In most church cultures of today, people do not want to 'get their hands dirty' by carrying one another's burdens, be they emotional, economic, physical, or spiritual. My challenge to the reader is: Do you reach out and touch?

In a day and age, when mental health issues are in ascendancy, where is the church? Very few mental health counselors are equipped to deal with the spiritual issues their clients bring to them. Many mental health counselors themselves are involved in occult-type beliefs, and some practice these beliefs in their own lives. How can they guide a person who is seeking the one true God and His ways in the path of righteousness? The blind cannot lead the blind. Also, the blind cannot give sight to those who are seeking to see. The demon-possessed cannot set the demon-possessed free. We need an accountable church. We need to leave the building, get out into the highways and byways as Jesus, St. Patrick, John Wesley, David Wilkerson, and many other missionaries have done over the years. We need to have the apostles and elders of the church gather people together and instruct them in the ways of the Lord. They need to lead the way. Praise the Lord that many people are not afraid to take Jesus to the streets in a variety of ways.

It is not just how many numbers are added to the church, but how the church is mentoring and teaching the new converts. Sunday school classes in most traditional churches have ceased to exist. Many churches no longer have a Sunday night or a midweek Bible study and/or prayer meeting. Is the church losing its power?

I do not think so. However, the church is losing its disciplines, and therefore, the church is no longer a New Testament body of believers across the land. Yes, some scattered believers walk and talk and practice the Kingdom of God that Jesus demonstrated while he was on earth. But consider this: among the people coming into the church today, could they stand firm during a time of severe persecution as did the early church under the Roman government? How would the church of Western culture react if its members were rounded up and threatened with death, or their family members threatened with death, if they did not deny Jesus?

In 2010, I was in Vietnam on a mission trip. I was honored to meet a pastor who mentored me in the ways of the church under that government. He shared some of his story with me. One night, the police of that government came to his house and brought him out into his yard. They told him they would kill him if he did not stop preaching the gospel and deny Jesus. He said he could not do that. His young son was awakened by the noise and came to an upstairs window and looked out. His wife and other children were in the yard watching. The pastor said he could not deny his Jesus. The authorities looked up at his young son in the window. They told the pastor that if he did not deny Jesus and stop preaching the gospel, they would set the house on fire with his son in it. Can you imagine this pastor's dilemma? What would you have done? The pastor was torn, and as he stood thinking about how to respond, his young son shouted to him, "Keep the faith, father. I am not afraid to die for Jesus." The man and the rest of his family stood and watched as the authorities set fire to the house and saw their child die. Is the church of the Western world this dedicated to the cause of Christ? We have not been asked to give up our physical lives for the Lord, even unto death. We are asked to give up all to follow him and share him with everyone we meet. Just sharing the gospel is not good enough. We must intimately engage people and share their burdens, their hopes, their joys, and their pain, so we can all stand firm in our faith together, and no one will be lost during the hard times. It is by sharing our lives that we learn to love as Christ commanded us to in John 15:12 and 17, *"A new command I give you. Love one another as I have loved you."* The church does not hate, ostracize, or grind into the soul of each other when they love one another as family.

Chapter 12:
Count the Cost

This section will explore how serious Jesus was about sharing the Kingdom of God with us and how serious we should be about sharing his kingdom with others. The charge we have been given is not to be taken lightly or frivolously. In Luke 14:25-27, 33, he has this to say:

Large crowds were traveling with Jesus, and turning to them, he said, "If anyone comes to me and does not hate father and mother, wife and children, brothers and sisters – yes, even their own life – such a person cannot be my disciple. And whoever does not carry their cross and follow me cannot be my disciple…In the same way, those of you who do not give up everything you have cannot be my disciples.

In the intervening verses, Jesus speaks of how when a person wants to build a tower, they sit down and count the cost of the project so they can bring it to completion. He then speaks of a king who is considering going to war and must take into consideration the size of the other king's army and how the battle can be fought and won. Jesus then says if the first king cannot figure out how to win the war, then he had better seek peace terms with the second king. In other words, if you want to be a disciple in the Kingdom of God, have you counted the cost? You have to be ready to do all that God would ask you to do. Are you ready to travel? Are you ready to go without? Are you ready to be uncomfortable at times? Are you ready to go someplace dangerous by society's standards? Are you ready to take risks? Are you ready to be made fun of? The list can go on and on, but you get the point. Following Jesus is not for those who shrink back. It is for soldiers who have taken an oath to follow their King wherever He sends them and do whatever He asks them to do. Following Jesus is a life-and-death walk. Yet, we do not walk it alone.

Serving in the army of the Lord will have its joys and its struggles. Yet, we will be at peace because we are obedient to the task set before us. Jesus told Peter to get out of the boat and walk toward him. As long as Peter kept his eyes on Jesus, he was able to defy nature, and liquid held him up. When he took his eyes off Jesus and looked at the sea surrounding him, he began to sink. When we commit to follow Jesus and teach and demonstrate the Kingdom of God to others, we have to be willing to keep our eyes on Jesus. He will keep us, protect us, and give us the love, compassion, and joy we need to demonstrate his care for humanity to others.

This walk does not happen overnight. It is a matter of being consistent in our desire to be all that God has designed us to be in His Kingdom. That desire will keep us focused on listening to the voice of the Holy Spirit as we are led, guided, and disciplined to prepare us to be good soldiers. During the last few hours of his life before the cross, Jesus shared how to be consistent disciples and how to bear the fruit we have been called to share with the world.

I am the true vine, and my Father is the gardener. He cuts off every branch in me that bears no fruit, while every branch that does bear fruit he prunes, so that it will be even more fruitful. You are already clean because of the word I have spoken to you. Remain in me, as I also remain in you. No branch can bear fruit by itself; it must remain in the vine. Neither can you bear fruit unless you remain in me. I am the vine; you are the branches. If you remain in me and I in you, you will bear much fruit; apart from me, you can do nothing. If you do not remain in me, you are like a branch that is thrown away and withers; such branches are picked up, thrown into the fire, and burned. If you remain in me and my words remain in you, ask whatever you wish, and it will be done for you. This is to my Father's glory, that you bear much fruit, showing yourselves to be my disciples. (John 15:1-8)

Once again, we are called to count the cost of being disciples of Jesus. Many feel that once you are saved, you are always saved.[18] The passage in John would suggest differently. Jesus is letting his disciples know that working for the Kingdom of God means getting ourselves into shape. It is a painful process. We all come to Jesus with our warts, our hurts, hates, and other human frailties of our old nature. This passage says that God is willing to take us on and clean us up so we are fit to serve in His Kingdom. But we must always keep our eyes on Jesus, spend time with him, listen to and learn his precepts. We all have fruit, but the purpose of being "pruned" by the Father is so we will have even more fruit evident in our lives. The promise of abiding and becoming more

---

[18] Over the years different explanations have been explored as to whether Judas Iscariot was "really saved." Yes, he was one of Jesus's 12 disciples. He was among the 12 who were sent out with "…power and authority to drive out all demons and to cure diseases, and he sent them to proclaim the kingdom of God and to heal the sick" (Luke 9:1b-2). However, we know from Luke 11:14-20, that when some people accused Jesus of driving out demons by Beelzebub, Jesus responded that "…a house divided against itself will fall…" Therefore, it can be deduced that at the time Judas was sent out with the other 11 disciples, he was following Jesus, listening to him, and being obedient to all he had learned. We do not know all the intimate details of Judas' decision to betray Jesus except in Luke 22:3 we have this statement: "Then Satan entered Judas, called Iscariot, one of the Twelve." The question then becomes, what had changed in Judas' heart and in his mindset of being committed to Jesus, that caused him to listen to the voice of Satan? Judas committed treason against the Son of God. In John 17:12b during Jesus' prayer he says, "…None has been lost except the one doomed to destruction so that Scripture would be fulfilled."

fruitful carries a richness that cannot be imagined. We can ask whatever we wish, and it will be done for us. The downside is that if we do not continue to abide, then we are cast aside, and the implication is that hell is waiting to receive those who do not abide. Being a disciple in the Kingdom of God demands total allegiance and willingness to follow the precepts and conditions laid down by the Father. His kingdom is not a pick-and-choose discipleship. We are in His army; He is our commanding officer. We are to obey without question. He is omnipotent and omnipresent, so we can trust that He knows us and all that He is calling us to do.

Once we have committed to doing as Jesus taught and demonstrated, submitting ourselves to His leading, and continuing to abide, we are ready to go into battle in the marketplace. What does the marketplace look like? Look around you. Where are you? Who do you see? Where do you shop? Where do you work? Where do you play? This is your marketplace, unless you are called by the Holy Spirit to go to a different marketplace. Your current marketplace contains people you know and who know you. Think about how if you totally submit to the Lordship of Jesus Christ, your life will be changed, and you will be a witness to those around you. They will know 'the before' and 'after' you. They will be your "hardest sell," so to speak. Yet, they will know that it is God alone who has brought about the change, and He will receive all the glory.[19] Everything we say and do is to bring glory to the Father. Jesus said in different places in the book of John that whatever he did was to the glory of the Father and whatever we do in his name is *"...so that the Father may be glorified in the Son"* (John 14:1-14; 15:8).

Let us return to the commission Jesus gave to the twelve disciples and also to the seventy-two other people, not disciples, but those who chose to follow Jesus during his earthly ministry. To the twelve whom he sent to the surrounding Judean countryside to minister to their Jewish brothers and sisters, he gave this instruction:

Take nothing for the journey – no staff, no bag, no bread, no money, no extra shirt. Whatever house you enter, stay there until you leave that town. If people do not welcome you, leave their town and shake the dust off your feet as a testimony against them. (Luke 9:3-5)

To the seventy-two who were sent into all the towns he was to later go into, both Jewish territory and Gentile regions, he gave these instructions and admonitions:

The harvest is plentiful, but the workers are few. Ask the Lord of the harvest, therefore, to send out workers into his harvest field. Go! I am sending you out like lambs among wolves. Do not take a

---

[19] Acts 9:1-29, The Story of Saul's conversion and his reception by the believers in the community

purse or a bag or sandals, and do not greet anyone on the road. When you enter a house, first say, "Peace to this house." If someone who promotes peace is there, your peace will rest on them; if not, it will return to you. Stay there, eating and drinking whatever they give you, for the worker deserves his wages. Do not move around from house to house. When you enter a town and are welcomed, eat what is offered to you. Heal the sick who are there and tell them, "The Kingdom of God has come near to you." But when you enter a town and are not welcomed, go into its streets and say, "Even the dust of your town we wipe from our feet as a warning to you. Yet be sure of this: The Kingdom of God has come near. (Luke10:1-11)

That brings us to present-day, twenty-first-century followers of Jesus. The call to follow Jesus, the commissioning to do as he did, has not changed. The workers are still few in number. When we go out today, we are outnumbered and surrounded by an unbelieving world. The Christians of today are still like lambs among wolves, who seek to silence the name of Jesus. This is not just in communist countries, but in what are considered the free countries of the world today. Christian Christmas displays are banned in some community parks and courthouse steps. Prayer is no longer an acceptable part of the school day as it was when I was a child, nor is the Lord's Prayer. The average person does not know the Ten Commandments, nor the Golden Rule. Under the surface, there is unrest, anger, hatred, and the belief that no one can tell us what to do because we "have rights." Things are only going to get worse before the great and marvelous coming day of the Lord. We, too, have been given a commission. We are told in Matthew 28:18-20:

Then Jesus came to them and said, "All authority in heaven and on earth has been given to me. Therefore, go and make disciples of all nations, baptizing them in the name of the Father and of the Son and of the Holy Spirit, and teaching them to obey everything I have commanded you. And surely I am with you always, to the end of the age.

Have you been equipped for the task we accepted our commission for? What else do you need? We will now turn to the book of Acts to discover how to move forward in the army of the Lord and to demonstrate the power of the Kingdom of God's glory to all.

Chapter 13:
Come, Holy Spirit

If you have ever had the privilege of being around someone who has been told they do not have long to live, you know that many times people begin to share things they wish they had said while they had all the time in the world. They share their inmost thoughts, their hearts, with their loved ones. (Of course, this is taking into consideration the family is not a dysfunctional one.) On the night he was betrayed, Jesus took quite a long while in sharing his heart with his family, his disciples. Throughout Chapter 14 of the gospel of John, Jesus tells his disciples he will not be with them much longer. We know that they did not completely understand what he was saying to them by the content of their questions. Despite their inability to totally comprehend all he was saying, he did tell them that he would *"... ask the Father, and he will give you another advocate to help you and be with you forever – the*

Spirit of truth…I will not leave you as orphans; I will come to you" (John 14:16-17a, 18).

Starting in chapter 12 of the book of John, we read that Jesus began to share openly that he was not going to be in the world much longer. What a shock this must have been to his disciples and those who were hearing his words. He had just come into Jerusalem and been given a king's reception by all the people who had gathered for the Passover feast. Now, here he was telling the disciples gathered in the upper room that he was leaving. Can you imagine what was going on in their minds, their emotions? Jesus is pouring his heart out to them. The time is short. We can only try to put ourselves in the disciples' place. Confusion, misunderstanding, perhaps fear, a sense of loss, but unsure how and the why of everything surrounding what he is saying will impact them. By the time Jesus completes the things he wants to say to them, he recognizes how impossible it is for them to fully comprehend what he is saying. In John 16:12-15, Jesus offers this word of comfort and promise to his disciples,

I have much more to say to you, more than you can now bear. But when he, the Spirit of truth, comes, he will guide you into all the truth. He will not speak on his own; he will speak only what he hears, and he will tell you what is yet to come. He will glorify me because it is from me that he will receive what he will make known to you. All that belongs to the Father is mine. That is why I said the Spirit will receive from me what he will make known to you.

We will now go to John 20:22-23. Jesus is resurrected and appears in a locked room *"…for fear of the Jewish leaders"* and stands among his disciples. The first words out of Jesus' mouth were *"Peace be with you!"* After showing them the scars on his hands and side, scripture tells us the disciples were overjoyed. Jesus then repeats the words, *"Peace be with you!"* Verses 22 and 23 then continue, *"And with that he breathed on them and said, 'Receive the Holy Spirit. If you forgive anyone's sins, their sins are forgiven; if you do not forgive them, they are not forgiven."* Jesus repeats the concept that if the disciples choose to forgive, then all the people who crucified Jesus, from the Jewish leaders, the Roman officials, down to the people who advocated for the release of the criminal Barabbas and the crucifixion of Jesus, would be forgiven. These disciples needed peace. Their lives, their worldview, their concept of who Jesus was as the Son of God, had been turned upside down. These were people who had the capacity to hate, to resent, to seek revenge, and so on. They had no peace, but Jesus gave them Shalom, peace, and the authority to forgive through the power of the Holy Spirit, whom he breathed on them.[20]

---

[20] Matthew 5:44 "But I tell you, love your enemies and pray for those who persecute you…" The Lord's Prayer (Matthew 6:9-13) includes the concept of forgiveness of others, as we ourselves have been forgiven.

Patricia C. Friel

The Gospel of John (21:15-19) concludes with Jesus restoring Peter to do kingdom work, after Peter had denied him three times on the night Jesus was arrested.[21] Luke (24:44-49), the recorder of the orderly account of all that happened to Jesus, tells us that Jesus, after his resurrection, appeared to the disciples and had this to say:

He said to them, "This is what I told you while I was still with you: Everything must be fulfilled that is written about me in the Law of Moses, the Prophets, and the Psalms. Then he opened their minds so they could understand the Scriptures. He told them, "This is what is written: The Messiah will suffer and rise from the dead on the third day, and repentance for the forgiveness of sins will be preached in his name to all nations, beginning at Jerusalem. You are witnesses of these things. I am going to send you what my

Ephesians 4:32 echoes this as Paul writes, "Be kind and compassionate to one another, forgiving each other, just as in Christ God forgave you." Matthew 6:14-15 makes it quite clear why it is important to practice forgiveness. "For if you forgive other people when they sin against you, your heavenly Father will also forgive you. But if you do not forgive others their sins, your Father will not forgive your sins." No one can truly forgive from their heart without the help of the Holy Spirit. The disciples had been through much, and Jesus was asking them to forgive. They needed the help of the Holy Spirit.

[21] Peter's denial of Jesus is found in all four gospels: Matthew 26:69-75; Mark 14:66-72; Luke 22:54-62; John 18:15-18, 25-27. Only John's Gospel records his restoration

Father has promised, but stay in the city until you have been clothed with power from on high.”[22]

Luke continues the story of Jesus and his last forty days on earth. The instructions that Jesus gave to his disciples during those last days are, as Luke records them in Acts 1:2, *“…through the Holy Spirit…”* Luke goes on to say in verse 3b that Jesus spoke to these disciples about the Kingdom of God. We do not know exactly what he may have included, but we do know what his final parting command was for them.

Do not leave Jerusalem, but wait for the gift my Father promised, which you have heard me speak about. For John baptized with water, but in a few days you will be baptized with the Holy Spirit. (Acts 1:4b-5) …But you will receive power when the Holy Spirit comes on you; and you will be my witnesses in Jerusalem, and in all Judea and Samaria, and to the ends of the earth. (Acts 1:8)[23]

---

[22] The word in Greek that is used for power is Dunamis, the same root word from which we derive the word dynamite. It is explosive power, moving things rapidly, and nothing can stand in its way.

[23] Tradition relates that Peter went to Rome, Greece, and Antioch. Andrew went to Greece, Asia Minor, modern Russia/Ukraine. Thomas went to India. Matthew went to Spain, France, Ethiopia, and Britain. Nathanael went to Turkey, Persia, and Ethiopia. Philip went to Turkey. Thaddeus went to Persia, Parthia, and Armenia. James, son of Zebedee went to Spain. James, son of Alphaeus and Simon the Zealot, went to Egypt, N. Africa, Persia, Middle East. Matthias, who replaced Judas Iscariot, went to the Middle East, Ethiopia, and Georgia.

As can be seen by these verses, something needed to happen in the lives of the disciples to motivate them, to embolden them, to set them on fire, so they could spread the Good News of the kingdom. They had repented, they had even been water baptized, but they were still afraid to share the Good News that Jesus had risen from the dead. They were in hiding for fear that the Jews and perhaps even the Romans would find them and execute them also. In a sense, we are no different today than the disciples of Jesus' day. Can you count how many people you have witnessed to in the last week, the last month, the last year, or even in your life? Why not? Are you afraid of being looked at differently? Are you afraid of social persecution? The list of questions could go on, but the answer is the same for us as it was for the disciples. We need the Holy Spirit to come upon us with power.

As scripture makes clear, the answer is a visitation of the Holy Spirit — one who comes to take up residence within us. We need the Holy Spirit to draw us to the feet of Jesus and aid in repentance, but the baptism of the Holy Spirit is a different work of grace in the life of the believer. There are two illustrations from the book of Acts that demonstrate that being baptized in water and being baptized in the Holy Spirit are two separate graces. The Holy Spirit is active in both graces, but the baptism with the Holy Spirit is where we receive the boldness and the power to live the Kingdom of God out on this earth in the here and now.

The story of Philip preaching and demonstrating the power of God to the Samaritans in Acts 8:4-17 illustrates that repentance followed by water baptism is a totally different grace than receiving the Holy Spirit. This fact is also borne out by the story of Cornelius in Acts 10:1-11:18. Pay particular attention to Acts 10:44-48 and Acts 11:15-18, as mentioned below.

While Peter was still speaking these words, the Holy Spirit came on all who heard the message. The circumcised believers who had come with Peter were astonished that the gift of the Holy Spirit had been poured out even on Gentiles. For they heard them speaking in tongues and praising God. Then Peter said, 'Surely no one can stand in the way of their being baptized with water. They have received the Holy Spirit just as we have. (Acts 10:44-48)

As I [Peter] began to speak, the Holy Spirit came on them as he had come on us at the beginning. Then I [Peter] remembered what the Lord had said: 'John baptized with water, but you will be baptized with the Holy Spirit.' So if God gave them the same gift he gave us who believed in the Lord Jesus Christ, who was I [Peter] to think that I could stand in God's way?' (Acts 11:15-18)

The evidence presented is the ability to speak in a language you have not learned. It is the language of the Trinity. It is a language given through the Holy Spirit, so you know he has baptized you with power to witness and live out the Kingdom of God on earth through witnessing, miracles, healings, and deliverance. This is a wonderful gift from God that keeps on giving and giving. It yields only positive returns.

Take this opportunity to pray and ask the Lord to baptize you in His Holy Spirit. Remember, this is the gift Jesus promised. We cannot do kingdom work without the Holy Spirit being alive and active in our lives.

Chapter 14:
Signs, Wonders, and Miracles

Jesus not only demonstrated the power of the Kingdom of God, but he told his disciples on the night he was betrayed in John 14:12-14 that:

Very truly I tell you, whoever believes in me will do the works I have been doing, and they will do even greater things than these, because I am going to the Father. And I will do whatever you ask in my name, so that the Father may be glorified in the Son. You may ask me for anything in my name, and I will do it. [Bold by author to highlight this truth]

The works Jesus demonstrated were not new. They were works the Father had already demonstrated through the prophets in the Old Testament. The people of Jesus' day should have been prepared when the Messiah came because they did have the Law and the writings of the prophets, whose job was to set the scene. Amazingly, those who should have been in the know, so to speak, teaching the people, appeared to be the least informed. This includes the teachers of the Law and the Pharisees. Yet, it was the person on the street, who was most receptive to Jesus' ministry. When Jesus began his ministry, he was able to demonstrate these works daily, a multiplicity of times each day. The gospel accounts give a sampling of the different types of signs, wonders, and miracles that Jesus performed for the Father's glory.[24] Jesus not only performed the same type of signs, wonders, and miracles as did the prophets, but he performed them in various modalities. He did even more than the prophets did.

The continuation of Jesus' ministry shows that *"Jesus is the same, yesterday, today, and forever"* (Hebrews 13:8). Also, Malachi 3:6 reminds us that *"I the LORD do not change."* In addition, James 1:17 has this to say about the Father,

Every good and perfect gift is from above, coming down from the Father of the heavenly lights, who does not change like shifting shadows.

From Chapter One of the Gospel of John, we know that Jesus, the Son, and God the Father are the same. The Apostle's Creed reminds us that we worship a Triune God, Father, Son, and Holy Spirit. Revelation 1:8 reminds us that "I am the Alpha and the

---

[24] John 21:25 says, "Jesus did many other things as well. If every one of them were written down, I suppose that even the whole world would not have room for the books that would be written."

Omega," says the Lord God, "who is, and who was, and who is to come, the Almighty."

I want to take some time to refresh what some of the signs, wonders, and miracles were that occurred in the Old Testament and then segue to the signs, wonders, and miracles of Jesus' ministry. The prophets did nothing that was hidden from the people, nor did Jesus. Crowds were present at almost every sign, wonder, and miracle in both Testaments. Some examples from the Old Testament include the healing of Naaman from leprosy (2 Kings 5:1-19). Naaman was the commander of the army. His whole entourage was present for his healing, encouraging him to do as the prophet Elisha had instructed. They saw him as leprous; they saw him after he had dipped in the water seven times, completely healed. Matthew 8:1-3 states that,

When Jesus came down from the mountain, large crowds followed him. A man with leprosy came and knelt before him and said, "Lord, if you are willing, you can make me clean." Jesus reached out his hand and touched the man. "I am willing," he said, "Be clean!"

It is difficult to categorize the signs, wonders, and miracles that occurred in both Testaments, but I think they can be placed in the following:

Nature signs, wonders, and miracles: The parting of the Red Sea so that Moses and the Children of Israel could pass over on dry land (Exodus 14:10-18).[25] Jesus and Peter walking on the water (Matthew 14:25-29). The water turned to wine (John 2:1-11)

Compassion signs, wonders, and miracles: Elisha restored a son to life (2 Kings 4:32-35). Jesus raised these people from the dead: Jairus the Pharisee's daughter (Matthew 9:18-19, 23-26), the widow of Nain's son (Luke 7:11-17), and his friend, Lazarus (John 11:1-44).

Miraculous physical births to women past child-bearing years: Sarah, the mother of Isaac (Genesis 17:11-12, 21:1-2), Elizabeth, the mother of John the Baptist (Luke 1:7, 18, 24).

Physical healing miracles: King Hezekiah's recovery (2 Kings 20:1-11).[26] A woman with a hemorrhage for twelve years (Mark 5:25-34).[27]

Spiritual healing miracles: Jonah's visit to the city of Nineveh and their repentance (Jonah Chapter 3), the paralyzed

---

[25] The book of Exodus from chapters 1-11 is a condensed saga of the miracles and wonders over the creation God had spoken into existence in Genesis chapter 1. The animal kingdom, the insect kingdom, the waters turning to blood with death to the fish and amphibians, the plant kingdom when the burning bush was not consumed, the weather, over the lights that 'governed the day and the night', and over the life of humankind itself in boils, and the death of the firstborn.

[26] There are many physical healings in the Old Testament that I will list in the appendix in the back of this book.

[27] There are so many healing miracles of Jesus that can be read in the gospel accounts that I am not going to try to recount all of them in this chapter. Please see the appendix at the end of this book.

man brought by his four friends (Mark 2:1-5), Peter's restoration after denying Jesus three times (John 21:15-17).

Deliverance signs, wonders, and miracles: King Saul's tormenting spirit was not healed but was soothed by David playing the harp (1 Samuel 16:23). Jesus often met the demonic, and the evil spirits were cast out, not just soothed (Matthew 8:16).

Judgment signs, wonders, and miracles: Elijah confronted the 450 prophets of Baal during King Ahab's reign (1 Kings 18:16-40). The death of Ananias and Sapphira for lying to Peter and the rest of the apostles (Acts 5:1-11).

Whether in the Old Testament or the New Testament, signs, wonders, and miracles confirm the bona fides that God is who He says He is, the Creator of the heavens and the earth and all that is within them. He has not changed His ways throughout history. He continues to prove Himself over and over again to a people who have rebellion written on their hearts from the father of lies himself, the devil. Satan is forever deceiving people into believing that he holds power to prove he is just like God. Jesus demonstrated that Satan's power is fleeting and robs people of health, spiritual freedom, and leads them to death. Jesus said in John 10:10, *"The thief comes only to steal and kill and destroy; I have come that they may have life, and have it to the full."*

Jesus announced that the Kingdom of God has come. He taught about the Kingdom of God, and he demonstrated the

Kingdom of God to everyone by signs, wonders, and miracles. He took authority over the satanic spirits. Even they knew who Jesus was and would declare the Lordship of Jesus in the midst of crowds of people who thronged his ministry (Luke 8:27-31).

When Jesus stepped ashore (in the region of the Gadarenes), he was met by a demon-possessed man from the town. For a long time, this man had not worn clothes or lived in a house, but had lived in the tombs. When he saw Jesus, he cried out and fell at his feet, shouting at the top of his voice, "What do you want with me, Jesus, Son of the Most High God? I beg you, don't torture me!" For Jesus had commanded the impure spirit to come out of the man. Many times it had seized him, and though he was chained hand and foot and kept under guard, he had broken his chains and had been driven by the demon into solitary places. Jesus asked him, "What is your name?" "Legion," he replied, because many demons had gone into him. And they begged Jesus repeatedly not to order them to go into the Abyss.

Some in the church today do not want to become involved in the ministry of the Kingdom of God. They rationalize that it was just for Jesus and the first-century disciples to get the church of Jesus off to a good start. Others do not want to be known for being a fanatical Christian. Still others do not want to pay the price of being a committed follower of Jesus Christ, teaching, preaching, and demonstrating the Kingdom of God on earth today.

There is a price to pay for being a disciple in God's kingdom today, just as there was in Old Testament and New Testament times. Satan is still trying to stifle people from having an intimate relationship with God. The devil will lie to you and tell you that you are not good enough. He will tell you that everything Jesus taught and did is not necessary to share with others; they will laugh at you if you try. Just keep your faith to yourself. Jesus tells his disciples to count the cost of following him in Luke 14:25-27:

Large crowds were traveling with Jesus, and turning to them he said: "If anyone comes to me and does not hate his father and mother, wife and children, brothers and sisters – yes, even their own life – such a person cannot be my disciple. And whoever does not carry their cross and follow me cannot be my disciple.

He then goes on to give illustrations that, in the natural world, such as building a house or going to war, a person considers all the angles to determine the cost of the venture. He is asking all of us to count the cost before committing to following him and teaching and demonstrating the Kingdom of God to the world. Our lives and our conduct must be congruent at all levels. We must be people of integrity to declare the Kingdom of God to a lost and hurting world. The Holy Spirit will baptize us and enable us to do the Father's will, just as the Holy Spirit did for Jesus. Are you willing to *"…Love the Lord with all your heart and with all your soul and*

Patricia C. Friel

with all your mind and with all your strength...and to Love your neighbor as yourself" (Mark 12:28-31 full passage).[28]

---

[28] Then one of the scribes [an expert in Mosaic Law] came up and listened to them arguing [with one another], and noticing that Jesus answered them well, asked Him, "Which commandment is first and most important of all?" Jesus answered, "The first and most important one is: 'HEAR, O ISRAEL, THE LORD OUR GOD IS ONE LORD; AND YOU SHALL LOVE THE LORD YOUR GOD WITH ALL YOUR HEART, AND WITH ALL YOUR SOUL (life), AND WITH ALL YOUR MIND (thought, understanding), AND WITH ALL YOUR STRENGTH.' This is the second: 'YOU SHALL [unselfishly] 'LOVE YOUR NEIGHBOR AS YOURSELF.' There is no other commandment greater than these. The scribe said to Him, "Admirably answered, Teacher; You truthfully state that HE IS ONE, AND THERE IS NO OTHER BUT HIM; AND TO LIVE HIM WITH ALL THE HEART AND WITH ALL THE UNDERSTANDING AND WITH ALL THE STRENGTH, AND TO [unselfishly] LOVE ONE'S NEIGHBOR AS ONESELF, is much more than all burnt offerings and sacrifices." (Amplified Bible: Mark 12:28-33)

Chapter 15:
Walking in Kingdom Authority

This chapter will recap the order we need to do things in to be able to walk in the authority that Jesus gave to us as his disciples to a hurting and confused world. A world that wants to experience peace. A world that yearns to know they are loved by someone who created them, even if they do not get it from any place or anyone else.

The first step is to admit you are a sinner and that Jesus came to earth to die as the sacrificial lamb that *"takes away the sins of the world"* (John 1:29b). We then need to

acknowledge and confess with your mouth that Jesus is Lord [recognizing His power, authority, and majesty as God], and believe in your heart that God raised Him from the dead, you will be saved. For with the heart a person believes [in Christ as Savior], resulting in his justification [that is – being made righteous—being freed of the guilt of sin and made acceptable to

God]; and with the mouth he acknowledges and confesses [his faith openly], resulting in and confirming [his] salvation. (Romans 10:9-10 Amplified Bible)[29]

After we have asked Jesus to forgive us of our sins and believe that he has done so according to the Word of God, then we need to pray and ask him to fill us with his Holy Spirit. We are no different than Jesus himself, for Matthew 3:16 says, *"As soon as Jesus was baptized, he went up out of the water. At that moment heaven was opened, and he saw the Spirit of God descending like a dove and alighting on him."*

Several other scriptures deal with the necessity of waiting to be baptized with the Holy Spirit for ministry. Luke 4:1 lets us know that Jesus was able to fast and pray and withstand the temptations put to him by Satan because he was *"full of the Spirit."* Then, in Luke 4:14, scripture relates that Jesus returned to Galilee *"in the power of the Spirit."* In John 14:15-17, Jesus, on the night of his betrayal, tells his disciples:

If you love me, keep my commands. And I will ask the Father, and he will give you another advocate to help you and be with you forever – the Spirit of truth. The world cannot accept him, because it neither sees him nor knows him. But you will know him, for he lives with you and will be in you.

---

[29] Some Cross References: John 3:16; 11:25-26. Ephesians 2:8-9. Isaiah 45:22-23. Joel 2:32.

Jesus spent forty days after his resurrection with the apostles he had chosen and spoke about the Kingdom of God with them. Acts 1:4-5, 8 relates his final instruction to them.

Do not leave Jerusalem, but wait for the gift my Father promised, which you have heard me speak about. For John baptized with water, but in a few days you will be baptized with the Holy Spirit…you will receive power when the Holy Spirit comes on you; and you will be my witnesses in Jerusalem, and in all Judea, and Samaria, and to the ends of the earth.

It was not until after the Day of Pentecost (Acts 2:1-4) that the disciples and others who had gathered together to wait and pray for the Holy Spirit began to operate as the Kingdom of God on earth was meant to operate. The book of Acts tells of the miracles that were done through the Holy Spirit, the boldness with which they spoke the name of Jesus to all (Acts 4:8-14), and how they now recognized that it was the Holy Spirit that Jesus had promised that enabled them to do these things. After Peter and John were released and returned to their home, they, along with the other believers, prayed this prayer:

…Now, Lord, consider their threats and enable your servants to speak your word with great boldness. Stretch out your hand to heal and perform signs and wonders through the name of your holy servant, Jesus. (Acts 4:29-30)

The gift of the Holy Spirit of God, given through Jesus, is the beginning of bringing the Kingdom of God to a hurting world today, just as it was in the days of the early church. My challenge to all who read this is, if you have not been baptized in the Holy Spirit, wait, pray, and Jesus will give you this wonderful gift so you can be his witnesses here on earth. You, too, will operate in signs, wonders, and miracles.

If you have already been baptized in the Holy Spirit, with evidence of speaking in tongues, that is your prayer language that Satan cannot understand – but if you are not yet operating in signs, wonders, and miracles, I urge you to come into agreement with other Spirit-filled Christians and be refilled. It could be that you are depleted physically, mentally, and/or emotionally. We are baptized once with the Holy Spirit, but need to draw apart and be refilled. Acts 4:31 emphasized this.

After they had prayed, the place where they were meeting was shaken. And they were all filled with the Holy Spirit and spoke the word of God boldly.

Just as we are called to remember our water baptism, so we are called to come, sit at the feet of Jesus, and be filled to overflowing by his Holy Spirit to be witnesses, to be carriers of the Kingdom of God.

The Bible tells us in Psalm 37:4 that we are to *"Take delight in the LORD, and he will give us the desires of our heart."* Do you desire to bring the Kingdom of God to others? Are you willing to pay the price, whether personally, professionally, and/or spiritually? Praise the Lord! May His kingdom explode with dedicated workers. May His will be done on earth as it is in Heaven.

Patricia C. Friel

These are but very few of the various types of miracles found in both testaments. There are many more than listed in the chapter and in this chart. The challenge to the reader is, how many more can you identify? How would you categorize them?

Appendix

Category	Miracle/Event	Testament	Scripture Reference
Nature	All creation stories	Old Testament	Genesis
	Exodus of the children of Israel from Egypt	Old Testament	Exodus
	Sun and Moon stood still	Old Testament	Joshua 10:12-14
	Drought ordered by Elijah	Old Testament	1 Kings 17:1; James 5:17
	Ax head caused to float by	Old Testament	2 Kings 6:5-7
	Shadow goes back 20 degrees on sundial	Old Testament	2 Kings 20:9-11
	Preservation of Jonah in the belly of a great fish	Old Testament	Jonah 2:1-10
	Calming the storm	New Testament	Matthew 8:23-27; Mark 4:35-41; Luke 8:22-25

	Walking on the water	New Testament	Matthew 14:22-33; Mark 6:45-52; John 6:16-21
	Earthquake released Paul and Silas from prison	New Testament	Acts 16:25-26
Compassion	Manna sent from heaven in the Wilderness	Old Testament	Exodus 16:14-35
	Elijah fed by the ravens	Old Testament	I Kings 17:4-6
	Widow's oil and meal supernaturally increased	Old Testament	I Kings 17:12-16
	Shunammites' son raised from the dead	Old Testament	2 Kings 4:19-37
	Widow's son raised from the dead	Old Testament	I Kings 17:17-24
	Hundreds fed with 20 loaves	Old Testament	2 Kings 4:43-44
	Widow of Nain's son raised from the dead	New Testament	Luke 7:11-17
	Jairus's daughter raised from the dead	New Testament	Matthew 9:18-25; Mark 5:22-42; Luke 8:41-56
	Feeding of 5000	New Testament	Matthew 14:15-21; Mark 6:35-44 Luke 9:12-17; John 6:5-14
	Feeding of the 4000	New Testament	Matthew15:29-39; Mark 8:1-10
	Lazarus raised from the dead	New Testament	John 11:1-44
	Dorcas restored to life	New Testament	Acts 9:40

	Eutychus restored to life	New Testament	Acts 20:7-12
Miraculous Birth	Birth of Isaac to Sarah and Abraham	Old Testament	Genesis 21:1-7
	Samuel's mother prayed for a son	Old Testament	1 Samuel 1
	The Virgin Birth of Jesus	New Testament	Matthew 1:18-25; Luke 1 26-38
	Elizaeth becoming pregnant with John the Baptist	New Testament	Luke 1:6-7
Physical Healing	Naaman cured of leprosy	Old Testament	2 Kings 5:10-14
	Hezekiah healed after praying to God	Old Testament	2 Kings 20:7
	A royal official's son is healed in Cana	New Testament	John 4:46-54
	Healing of Peter's mother-in-law	New Testament	Matthew 8:14-15; Mark 1:29-31; Luke 4:38-39
	Evening spent healing the sick	New Testament	Matthew 8:16; Mark 1:32; Luke 4:40
	Healing of the woman with an issue of blood	New Testament	Matthew 9:20-22; Mark 5:25-34; Luke 8:43-48
	Blind man healed	New Testament	Mark 8:22-26
	Woman with a bad back	New Testament	Luke 13:10-13
	Malchus' severed ear restored	New Testament	Luke 22:45-54

	Many sick people healed by Peter	New Testament	Acts 5:12-16
	Lame man healed by Paul	New Testament	Acts 14:10
Spiritual Healing	Elijah taken up to heaven in a chariot of fire	Old Testament	2 Kings 2:11
	Four friends bring lame man to Jesus	New Testament	Matthew 9:1-8; Mark 2:1-12; Luke 5:17-26
	Jesus forgives and restores Peter	New Testament	John 21:15-19
	Dying Steven's vision of Jesus	New Testament	Acts 7:55-56
Deliverance	Three guys delivered from the fiery furnace	Old Testament	Daniel 3:19-27
	Daniel delivered from the lion's den	Old Testament	Daniel 6:16-23
	Healing of demon-possessed man	New Testament	Matthew 8:28-34; Mark 5:1-13; Luke 8:26-33
	Mute spirit cast out in Capernaum	New Testament	Matthew 9:32-33
	Healing of blind and mute man with demon	New Testament	Matthew 12:22-23; Luke 11:14
	Syro-Phoenician woman's daughter freed	New Testament	Matthew 15:21-28; Mark 7:24-30
	Two occasions when apostles freed from prison	New Testament	Acts 5:19; 12:7-11
Judgment	Cities of Sodom and Gomorrah destroyed	Old Testament	Genesis 19:24-25 and Lot's wife verse 26

	Nadab and Abihu destroyed	Old Testament	Leviticus 10:1-2
	Israel's judgment by fire	Old Testament	Numbers 11:1-3
	Two hundred and fifty men consumed by fire at Kadesh	Old Testament	Numbers 16:35-45
	Dagon's fall before the Ark, diseases affect Philistines	Old Testament	1 Samuel 5:1-12
	Young men mocked Elisha and torn by bears	Old Testament	2 Kings 2:24
	Death of Ananias and Sapphire	New Testament	Acts 5:1-11
	John's vision on the Island of Patmos	New Testament	Book of Revelation

About the Author

Miss Pat, as she is known in her community, has been in the mental health and substance abuse counseling fields since 1998. Her work has been with people from all walks of life, from nursing homes, long-term behavioral health inpatient facilities, halfway houses, re-entry, the homeless population, outpatient, and as a volunteer chaplain at a hospital in various departments. She completed her doctorate in 2023 from United Theological Seminary in Dayton, Ohio. Before entering United, she had been invited to Kenya to lead a three-day women's conference. On the plane ride home, she inquired of the Lord why He had sent her to Kenya. The response was to go to seminary and write. This book is the result of that instruction.

Miss Pat is also involved in ministry throughout the United States and overseas. Long before seminary, the Holy Spirit kept prompting her to read how Jesus taught and demonstrated the Kingdom of God while he was present on the earth. During a seminary class one night, this was voiced to the class at large, along with a question: "Why isn't this happening today?" Another classmate started to laugh and stated she needed to talk to Ken Fish. When the question went out, "Who is Ken Fish?" a gentleman spoke up and stated he was. He invited her to go to Toledo, Ohio, where he was holding a meeting. There, she saw the Kingdom of God in operation as Jesus taught and demonstrated.

In 1990, while reading a book entitled *The Cross and the Switchblade*, by David Wilkerson, the Spirit of the Lord put a hunger deep within her inmost being to minister to the population Rev. Wilkerson was talking about. A trip to New York City a few weeks later to engage with his ministry there sealed what she was to do. That led from being the Director of Discipleship of a large member church to obtaining a master's degree in mental health counseling from Wright State University. In 2008, the scripture from Luke 4:18-19 was burned into her heart as a call to ministry outside the walls of the traditional church building.

God has never failed to open doors of ministry with signs, wonders, and miracles following in her life since that time. Because of His miraculous kindness and mercy operative in her life, Miss Pat was led to purchase a commercial office building for the counseling practice. There, the Lord caused the majority of the staff, who were Christians, to begin to pray for clients as they would ask. Then, just before graduation from seminary in 2023, the Lord led Miss Pat to sell the property and the counseling practice. As a result, she was able to begin to purchase homes to rent to people in the homeless shelter who could not pass a background check for other landlords. To date, eight properties house people who otherwise would not be able to obtain housing because of questionable backgrounds. In 2024, the Holy Spirit prompted Miss Pat to stop into the local radio station and offer to go on air with people who had been recipients of God's grace and mercy in their lives in miraculous ways. This show was a blessing to all who participated and to those who listened.

No matter where God has called her to minister, as a pastor, as a teacher in various churches, in her office, or overseas, God is so good. His mercies never cease and are fresh every morning. Everything that has come about is because of His love and kindness. He answered the deep longings and prayers of her heart to provide for those that the world has many times written off. She prays to continue to minister the love of God in practical and compassionate ways to whoever God brings into her path.